PROTECTING THE ALPHA

EMILIA ROSE

Cover Designer: Covers by Christian

Editor: Jovana Shirley, Unforeseen Editing, www.unforeseenediting.com

Emilia Rose

emiliarosewriting@gmail.com

To you.

CHAPTER 1

ISABELLA

*H*ot.
    Heavy.
Heaving.

Fingers trembling, eyes burning, neck scorching, I collapsed into the bathtub. Desperate to cool off. Desperate to ease all this pain. Desperate to stop feeling all this—this fiery vengeance rushing through every one of my bodily veins.

My body roasted in the frigid tub as sweat rolled down my forehead. I turned on the cold water, letting it pour out of the faucet and gush against the bare side of my neck, hoping to the Moon Goddess that it cooled me down.

Through teary eyes, I stared at the closed and locked bathroom door and caught glimmers of the moonlight shining into the dark room from the window. It must've been four a.m. I whimpered and rubbed my neck, the pain unbearable.

Goddess, help me.

Starting at my neck, every part of my body felt like it was in flames.

I hadn't been this hot since … since Roman had refused to mark me and I fell into heat.

But how could I be in heat again? Roman had already marked—

"Kylo," my wolf purred.

Thighs burning, I spread my legs in the bath in hopes to cool the blazing path to my core. The water must've almost been freezing, but I could only feel the feverish ache inside my body. When I squeezed my eyes closed to ease the pain, all I imagined was Kylo lying in the bath with me, his taut body between my legs, his cock buried deep inside of me, and his canines sinking into my neck.

"No," I growled at my wolf, shaking my head from side to side. *"Stop it."*

Barely a week had gone by since the night that Roman and I had spent with Kylo, the night he thrust himself inside of me and filled my tight pussy as Roman took me from behind. And I'd be a damn liar if I said I hadn't thought about it happening again, imagining Kylo taking control this time and forcing me to take his cum.

"Find mate," my wolf commanded. *"Find mate and let him mark us."*

I gripped the edges of the bath, body tensing. *"Stop it. Now."*

"Mate. We need to mate."

"Roman!" I screamed, sinking down further in the bath.

"Not Roman. My mate," my wolf said to me. *"Kylo."*

Water sloshed over the edge of the tub, the bath overflowing with nearly freezing water. The doorknob jiggled as Roman banged on the door and ordered me to let him into the room so he could help me. But as crazy as it sounded, I didn't trust myself not to sprint right past him, out of the house, and toward Kylo.

If Roman opened the door right now, my wolf would take full control of my body.

I'd do something with Kylo that I'd regret.

"Go away," I yelled back at him, knowing that I had just called for him. It sounded insane. *I* sounded insane. Tears streamed down my cheeks from the sheer amount of pain attacking my body. "Go away. I'll be okay."

"Isabella, let me in," Roman demanded. "Before I break this door down."

"Don't come in!" I pleaded. I stumbled out of the bathtub, slipping over the edge and landing on my hands and knees, and cursed, knowing that it'd leave a bruise on my knees—and it wouldn't be the fun kind.

"Isabella, open up," Roman growled, jiggling the door handle harder. "You're in pain."

"Please," I begged, staggering to the door in the sheet of bathwater covering our floor.

"Why can't I come in and help you?" he asked, banging against the door.

"Because I'm in heat!"

Though it was a mate's job to soothe pain, especially during heat, I ... I didn't want my wolf to hurt Roman just in an attempt to find Kylo and force him to mark me. I needed this heat and pain to disappear. Now.

"Kylo," my wolf whispered. *"Find him now."*

When Roman burst through the door, my wolf forced me to shift faster than ever before. I sprinted out of the room so fast that I knocked him on his ass and then continued right for our second-story bedroom window, forgoing all sense of running down the stairs and to the front door.

When I shoved my body through the glass, it shattered onto the ground underneath me as I swayed in the air by Roman's death grasp on my neck. He sank his teeth into the back of my neck and yanked me back into the room, throwing me onto the bed and growling in his wolf form.

"Did you think I'd let you run away from me?" he asked through the mind link.

3

Standing, I growled back at him as he stalked toward me. In the distance and through the woods, I listened to the howls of our packmates on their night runs around the property to secure the perimeter. Dolus hadn't been seen for a week, but I wasn't taking any chances.

"Let me leave," I said through the link, not even thinking about the words before I said them. It seemed like the heat had taken control of my wolf and wanted to desperately find the man I had supposedly been mated to for four thousand years.

Roman stared up at me with those golden eyes and then hopped up onto the bed with me. I lunged at him, but somehow, he snatched me by the back of the neck again and held me down, belly on the mattress. *"Shift."*

After struggling against him for another few moments, I growled and shifted under his body, my skin cooling a bit under his touch. He shifted behind me, still holding me down by the canines lodged into the back of my neck. I took deep breath after deep breath, slowly regaining both my composure and control of my wolf.

"Why are you in heat?" he asked me. *"We've mated."*

Tears streamed down my cheeks. "Kylo," I whispered. "She wants Kylo."

When the heat nearly disappeared—only a lingering ache left—I relaxed fully against the mattress and closed my eyes, a sudden tiredness overtaking my body. Roman pulled his teeth out of my neck and lay behind me on the bed, his naked body against mine. Though he stayed quiet, I could tell that he'd tensed when I said Kylo's name.

We had talked endlessly about my relationship with Kylo this past week, but this never came up. I never even thought about marking that man, and now … now, my wolf ached for it. It was as if they were mates in this lifetime too.

"I'm sorry," I whispered, turning over to face him. Instead of looking him in the eye, I stared at his perfectly sculpted chest and curled into him. "I'm so sorry if I hurt you. My wolf … she … I can't control her. And she wants … she wants his mark."

"Do you?" he asked softly, unsteadily grasping my waist.

Did I want Kylo's mark? Hell, I hadn't even thought about it yet. I just wanted to get through this damn war against Dolus and save the wolf species. The thought had crossed my mind once —*once*—after Roman asked us if my bond with Kylo was similar to my bond with him. But I had been too caught up with other stuff to give it much thought.

"I'm sorry," I whispered, my wolf not even allowing me to answer his question.

Instead of getting angry like I'd thought he would, Roman trailed his fingers on my face and laced them into my hair, scratching lightly and shushing me to sleep. "It's okay, my dear Isabella. You have a lot on your mind." He drew his nose up the side of my neck, against his mark. "If you don't want to tell me now, you don't have to. But … I want to know before it happens." He gulped. "I need to prepare myself to see you with someone else's mark on your neck."

The words came out so … so heartbreakingly sad.

My bond with Kylo had taken such a toll on Roman. I could see it in his eyes. He was tired.

I just hoped that didn't mean he'd be easily corrupted. I couldn't lose him. I couldn't fucking lose him. I loved this man more than I loved Kylo, and I would never, *ever* let him go and be blinded by such chaos.

"I'll always be here for you, no matter what," he whispered.

My stomach tightened at his words, an uneasy feeling sitting heavily inside of me. But … while I told myself I wouldn't let Roman get hurt in this mess, I was the one who had knocked him down tonight, the one who had wanted to find Kylo during that wave of heat. Roman was my mate, the mate the Moon Goddess had blessed me with before she even knew about Kylo. If I was willing to do that to Roman just to have Kylo mark me, what else would I do to him for Kylo?

Tears welled up in my eyes, yet I forced my eyes closed and shook my head. No, I couldn't think that way right now. I couldn't let the chaos and corruption around me affect the way I thought about my mate because once I let those thoughts slip into my mind, they would become part of me.

CHAPTER 2

ISABELLA

*L*ying in bed next to Roman, I stared up at the ceiling. Though the heat had worn me out, I couldn't seem to fall asleep. With loud and irritating thoughts racing through my mind, I turned over onto my stomach on the mattress and groaned into my pillow. While Roman slept, his arm slipped off me, but he quickly wrapped it around my waist and moved closer to me, mumbling something incoherent into my hair and smiling against me.

I intertwined my fingers with his and inhaled deeply, trying to sleep. I just wanted the thoughts to stop for one damn moment, so I could rest in peace. But all that ran through my mind was the Moon Goddess confined in one of Dolus's evil traps, unable to perform her duties to protect the werewolf species.

If we ended Dolus's corruption, we might be able to save her.

Yet Kylo, Roman, and I had come up with hundreds upon hundreds of ways to stop the chaos this past week, and nothing had seemed to hold up. Every time we had a theory, an idea, a mere thought, it never came to fruition. Something always either came up, didn't add up, or just wasn't feasible to do with the wolves we had at our disposal and the lack of knowledge we had of Dolus and his true powers.

Knowing that I wouldn't be able to sleep any longer, I kissed Roman and crawled out of bed to get some water downstairs and to go through a couple more plans. I needed to figure out something. I hated just waiting around for Dolus to come to us. But we knew nothing of him—absolutely nothing.

Turning on the downstairs light, I jumped when I saw Kylo standing in our kitchen. "Did I wake you, princess?" he asked, sipping on a glass of water. With a gray V-neck draped over his chest and a pair of loose washed jeans hanging from his hips, he smirked and leaned against the counter.

"What are you doing here?" I asked, scooting by him to grab a glass for myself and hoping to the Goddess that my wolf wouldn't wake up and decide that it was time to have her mate mark us. I turned on the faucet. "Shouldn't you be at your packhouse?"

Before I could utter another word, he pushed me against the counter from behind me, one hand around my throat and the other clutching my waist. He trailed his nose up against the bare side of my neck. "I could feel you, Isabella. Your wolf ..." he growled. "Goddess, your wolf was calling out to me, begging me to come to you, to *take* you."

Breath caught in my throat, I clutched on to the countertop and let the glass overfill in the sink, my fingers paling. "Kylo," I whispered, feeling my wolf start to awaken. "Please, I ... I ... please stop before I lose control. My wolf, she'll demand it from me."

His canines grazed against my neck, and I moaned. He pressed himself against me from behind, grinding his hard cock against my ass, teasing me just the way he knew I liked it. I closed my eyes and vowed that he wouldn't get to me this time.

He couldn't.

"Goddess, princess, those moans do something sinister to me,"

Kylo murmured against my neck, tilting my head back slightly and kissing my skin. "Moan for me again."

Heat gathering in my core, I let go of the death grip on the counter and moaned softly again, unable to even think straight. My vision clouded, and my mind fogged with pleasure as my wolf slowly ripped control from me.

"Kylo," I whispered, voice cracking.

"Yes, princess?" he murmured against me, sucking my skin between his teeth.

"We have to … to …"

"To?"

I had the urge to call for Roman, to scream at him to get his ass out of bed and come down to the kitchen, where Kylo was seconds away from taking me himself. His wolf must've been on edge all night too, because, while he had always been forward, we had come to a mutual agreement to keep our hands off each other unless we were with Roman.

He could tease me all day long, but he hadn't touched me this past week.

"To wait until Roman … until he gets up," I said between raspy breaths.

"I want you now."

It wasn't a thought, wasn't a request, wasn't even a question.

It was a demand from a ruthless alpha—an alpha who ached to claim his mate.

Inhaling deeply, I gathered all the strength inside of me and pushed him away. I didn't think I'd be able to handle him that close for much longer because I … I wanted to sink my canines in his neck and take him. Him being here just made me more anxious for it to be done already.

But I didn't want to just rush into it. Hell, I didn't even know if I wanted him to mark me. My wolf did—and she forced me into thinking that I did too. But I was too committed to Roman to ruin the bond I had with him. Sleeping with someone else and marking them were two different things. If Roman wasn't comfortable with me marking Kylo, then I had to hold back every urge.

Now wasn't the time to deal with mate drama either. We had a war to stop and a Moon Goddess to save.

After blowing out a deep breath, I crossed my arms over my chest to hide my hardened nipples, grabbed my glass of water, and walked backward and away from Kylo. He watched my every move with his fury-ridden gold eyes, canines still extended past his lips.

"Wait until Roman is awake," I said to him, the corner of my lips curled. "Then, maybe you'll get to taste me. Until then … we have work to do." I nodded to the stack of papers about Dolus and corruption on the dining room table.

Taking one last step back, I bumped into someone's chest.

"And what kind of work is that?" Roman asked amusedly behind me, possessively wrapping his arm around my waist and drawing a finger up the column of my neck. "Hmm?"

"Roman, I—"

"Answer me, Isabella," he murmured against my ear, eyes flickering to Kylo. "The kind that lands you on your knees perhaps?"

CHAPTER 3

ISABELLA

"We were just, um …" I glanced at Kylo, feeling my heart race faster and faster when I thought about the way he'd pushed me against the counter a few moments ago and told me that he wanted to sink his teeth into my neck. "We weren't going to do anything like that."

Roman snaked his hand around my throat from behind, strumming his fingers up the column of my neck, and growled low in my ear, his canines pricking at the scars from his mark. "Are you sure about that? Because Kylo over there looks like he's about to pounce on you and take *what is mine.*"

I swallowed hard, heat warming my core, and pressed back against him, already noticing the bulge in his sweatpants. My breath caught in the back of my throat at how hard he was. No matter what I thought he felt about Kylo and me … he loved it. He loved exuding his dominance, and I loved when he did it too.

"Hmm?" Roman said against my ear, tilting my head to the side and tightening his grip around my throat. "Is that what this *work* was really going to be? Did you want him to bend you over our dining room table and take you from behind?"

Reaching behind me, I grasped him through his pants and wrapped my hand around him. He pushed his hips forward slightly, telling me that he wanted more of this, that he wanted to show Kylo who I really submitted to.

"Keep stroking my cock, baby," Roman grunted, staring over my shoulder at Kylo to taunt him like no other. "Show Kylo whose cock you choke on every night."

As the heat gathered in my core, I pressed my thighs together and clenched, continuing to stroke Roman's cock behind me. I trailed my fingers up and down his length, flicking them lightly across the head of his cock, right where he loved it.

He tightened his grip on me and pulled me closer. "He wants to mark you."

I stroked Roman faster at the thought, my heart pounding.

"Tell him that if he wants to mark your pretty little neck, he has to work for it," Roman murmured into my ear, sucking my earlobe between his teeth and tugging on it gently, his stubble tickling my neck.

My lips parted, yet no words came out. All I could focus on was my ragged breath and the growing bulge in Kylo's jeans, pressing against the material and making it tight on his thighs. He stood by the kitchen counter, palms on it behind him and biceps flexing.

"Tell. Him. Now."

"No," I said in defiance.

Roman growled against me, "Show him this neck." Roman cupped my chin and tilted my head to the side, so Kylo had a clear view of the bare side of my neck. "Show him what he can't have yet. Let him smell you there, taste you there, and then tell him no, Isabella, because if you can't obey a simple request, you don't get marked tonight."

Roman was taunting him—full-on fucking taunting another alpha.

My eyes widened, and my pussy clenched. "Touch me," I whispered. "But don't mark me. Not yet."

As if he didn't need to be told twice, Kylo sauntered over to me, wrapped one hand around my waist, and dipped the other between my legs. Then, he buried his face into the crook of my neck, inhaling my scent and pressing his full lips against my aching skin.

Moaning, I pulled Roman's cock out of his pants and gripped it tighter. Kylo rubbed his fingers against my clit in torturous little circles, making my legs tremble. I curled my toes and looked over my shoulder at Roman.

"Give it to me," I pleaded. As much as I wanted to push him away and make *him* work for it, I ached for him to be inside me already, needed him to fill my tight little hole up with his cock and his cum. "Please, Roman."

After pushing down my pants, Roman spit on his cock and rubbed his head against my pussy, making it even wetter with my juices. Holding me upright with one hand around my jaw and the other around my waist, he slowly pushed himself inside of me. Pleasure rushing through my body from Kylo's fingers, I clenched on Roman and arched my back, allowing Kylo even better access to my neck.

At the base of my neck, he sucked on my skin, grunting and growling low to himself, his wolf so close to the edge.

Roman shoved into me from behind, cursing in my ear and shoving himself deeper each time. "Fuck, Isabella, you're so fucking tight for me."

With each thrust, he sent me closer and closer to Kylo. And when Kylo grazed his canines against my neck, my breath caught in the back of my throat. I curled my toes, thinking about him sinking his teeth into my neck and claiming me himself, right here and right now. My wolf and I would be pleased. Yet before he could claim me, Roman pushed his hand between Kylo's teeth and my neck, sprawling his palm and fingers around my throat so Kylo had no room to bite me.

But it was too late to stop Kylo's wolf. Kylo clamped down his teeth, piercing Roman's fingers instead of my neck. Roman howled ruthlessly and shoved him backward so violently that he slammed against the kitchen island. Kylo flew back, his eyes golden, as if he had no control over his body anymore, and his sharp canines lengthened fully.

"Punish him for trying to mark you after you told him no," Roman said, sucking the blood off his fingers so it wouldn't ruin our carpet, continuing to pound into me from behind even harder and faster, more ruthlessly somehow.

"Punish him?" I asked with wide eyes, heat crawling up my neck.

"Just like I punish your bratty"—thrust—"fucking"—thrust— "ass."

Before I could shut my mouth in defiance, I found myself pulling out a dining room chair and demanding that Kylo sit on it. Once he did, I pulled his cock out of his pants, knelt before him with Roman still buried deep inside of me, and stroked him slowly.

"Don't come," I ordered him, placing my hands on his thighs and bending over further so Roman could ram into me from behind. I wrapped my hand around the base of Kylo's cock. "And don't touch me either. You only get to watch."

I lowered my head and took the head of his cock into my mouth. By the way his hips twitched slightly when my lips met the base of his hips, I could tell that he was already close to the edge, just like I was. I stared up at him, feeling my insides flutter at the control I had over this man, and slowly bobbed my head.

Roman curled his fingers into my hips from behind and pounded harder into me. "Fuckin' harder," he ordered, grabbing my hair and forcing me to bob my head on his cock.

And just before Kylo was about to come, Roman pulled me back.

"Don't come," I said to Kylo.

When he relaxed, I sucked his dick into my mouth, bobbing my head up and down on him until his hips twitched again and he stilled. Before he could come, I pulled back up and teased his balls with my tongue.

"Don't. Come."

"Fuuuck, Isabella," Kylo said to me, balling his hands into fists.

Roman curled one arm around my waist to rub my clit and leaned down closer to me. "Kylo might not be allowed to come, but you're going to come with his cock in your mouth. Do you understand me?"

I clenched down hard on Roman's cock and nodded, staring back at Kylo and wrapping my lips back around his head. I bobbed my head up and down on him and tightened harder and harder around Roman. Roman rubbed my clit faster, grabbed a fistful of my hair again, and forced me down as far as I could go on Kylo's cock. I stared up at Kylo with watery eyes, feeling his hips twitch again.

He was going to come.

"Don't come," I tried saying with his cock in my throat, but it came out as nothing but slobbery gargles.

He rolled his eyes back and lifted his hips to get even deeper in my throat. Roman shoved himself into me. And at the same time, they both came inside of me, Kylo's cum shooting down my throat and Roman's filling me up. I gagged on Kylo's cum and smacked my hands against his thighs, screaming out on his cock as I came all over Roman.

Yet Roman still held me down on him, pushing his cum deeper toward my cervix. When he finally let me go, I pulled my head up to gasp for breath and moan, my legs trembling uncontrollably. Roman scooped me into his arms so I wouldn't fall over and set me in a chair beside Kylo.

15

"You need to learn how to be a better domme, Isabella," Roman said, trailing his thumb down my lips. "You told him not to come and then let him come anyway."

"I-I-I couldn't help it," I said, pulling my knees to my chest as the pleasure still pumped through me. I sucked in a deep breath. "Maybe next time."

CHAPTER 4

ISABELLA

*A*fter our lovely morning in the packhouse, I packed up some notes, journals, and maps into my backpack, grabbed Roman's hand, and led him and Kylo to the hospital. Since the attack, I had been visiting the hospital with them every morning to check on Vanessa. If I went alone, I'd start crying my eyes out.

When I stepped into the hospital, Mom greeted me at the counter with her hands in her white jacket pockets. "Morning, sweetie," she said, glancing at Kylo trailing behind us.

I hadn't really told her about my connection with him yet because I didn't know how to say it. It wasn't usual to have two mates, never mind be one of the two original divine wolves.

"Hi, Mom," I said, tugging Roman along toward Vanessa's room. "How's Vanessa?"

"Better than yesterday," she said with a smile, glancing back and forth between the three of us. She nodded to the other side of the room. "Izzy, can I talk to you for a second? In private? There are some things I need to speak with you about."

Though I didn't want to have this conversation, I let go of Roman's hand and walked to the other side of the room with her.

17

Being werewolves with improved hearing, we never really had any kind of privacy, but this would have to do.

She glanced at me and then at my mates. "What's going on with you and Alpha Kylo? People in this pack have been whispering about you three, and I don't want them spreading lies about my baby."

I arched a brow, wondering who the hell had been whispering about us, and then sighed. "We're just ... friends?" I said, more as a question. Not because I didn't want Kylo, but because I didn't want to label us. Things were already messy as they were—hell, I'd wanted him to *mark me* this morning. Labeling us would just ... confuse things even more.

This way, I at least had some control of my wolf.

Some.

"Friends?" Mom asked, crossing her arms over her chest as if she didn't believe me. "Well, your father wants to meet this *friend* of yours. Invite him to dinner this week along with you and Roman." Before she let me go, she grasped my wrist and pulled me in closer. "And, Izzy, friends don't look at each other like you two do. I've seen that look before when you and Roman—"

"Okay, Mom," I said, pushing her away slightly. "I get it. I get it."

She rocked back on her heels with a huge smile on her face. "I'm sure you are getting it."

I scrunched my nose and glanced back at my guys. Roman leaned against one of the walls, one foot kicked up against it, while Kylo sat on a bench, his forearms rested against his thighs. When I glanced at them, they stopped talking and looked back at me almost as if on cue. My cheeks flamed as I remembered this morning.

Domme-ing wasn't my forte. I was a brat by nature. But, Goddess, I loved doing it to Kylo even though I was nervous about it. I didn't want to say the wrong thing or hurt him or

18

make him feel like I didn't care much about him. Yet seeing him so willing to please me made me … shiver in delight.

"Oh Goddess," Mom said, ushering me back to the guys. "You're in love."

"Shush it," I said to her, not wanting everyone to hear, especially my wolf. If my wolf knew I felt for Kylo almost as much as she did, she'd be even more aggressive than she was now and make me do something that I'd regret later.

After excusing myself from the conversation with Mom, I snatched up Roman's hand again and walked with them down the hall to Vanessa's room. I peeked into the room through the door window and nearly shrieked when I saw her moving.

"Vanessa!" I said, hurrying into the room and enveloping her in my arms—gently, of course. "Thank the Goddess you're awake!"

Vanessa stared at me with wide eyes, not moving as much as I had hoped, and pushed herself to a seated position with trembling arms. "Is-Is-Isa …" she desperately tried to get out, her voice raspy.

I grabbed a water bottle from my backpack and placed it against her lips. She drank it hungrily, gulping the entire water bottle down before I could even pull it away.

After licking her dry lips, she glanced around the room at Roman and Kylo. "You're all … all here. I didn't … die."

Scooting into the bed with her, I stroked her blonde hair and smiled. "No, you didn't die. Kylo rushed you to the hospital," I said, smiling at Kylo, who stood by Roman at the foot of the bed.

They both gave her a tense half-smile and whispered something back and forth, but I didn't have the time or the energy to give it much thought.

"How do you feel?" I asked her, brows furrowed.

"Like shit." She sat back and glanced over at the table by the window with papers about Dolus scattered all over it. "What's that?"

"We, uh, sometimes work here during the day."

"*You* work here," Roman said. "All hours of the night too."

I beamed and pulled her closer to me again. "You're one of my friends. I wanted to make sure you were getting the best treatment, and I wanted to be here when you woke up."

Vanessa grinned at me, but a moment later, she dropped her smile. "Hey, I'm sorry about what happened when we got ice cream the other night when I tried to kiss you. I couldn't help it, and I … I'm sorry. I overstepped. I shouldn't have done what I did."

"It's okay," I whispered, tucking some hair behind her ear. "I'm just glad that you're safe and healing now. I don't know what I would do without you."

Kylo grabbed my backpack from my shoulders and placed it on the table beside the window, glancing outside as the rain pounded against the trees. Not only had Dolus gone missing for the past week, but this weather had been crazy. It was almost as if this was his fucked up way of getting us not to find him. Not many wolves wanted to run in the rain, but my pack had done it numerous times during war before. We would do it again if we had to.

"Enough with the chitchat," Roman said, nodding to the table. "We have to work. Dolus is still out there."

CHAPTER 5

ROMAN

*S*itting on the edge of Vanessa's hospital bed, I watched Isabella crease her forehead and gnaw on her cheek, like she always did when she was worried. My lips curled into a soft smile, and I reached forward to tuck some loose strands of her brown hair behind her ear.

"We'll do it, Isabella. We'll get Dolus. Don't panic."

Isabella glanced over at me with big, bothered eyes but then nodded. "I know. I'm just … stressed." She glanced over my shoulder at Vanessa, who was sound asleep and snoring softly, and then Isabella sighed and sat beside me, lacing her fingers around mine. "I'm stressed about Dolus but also this morning."

"Kylo," I said, tightening my grip on her.

Kylo had left two hours ago to train with his pack and prepare them for the war ahead as Isabella and I stayed here to work and bounce ideas off each other—more ideas that honestly hadn't caught on. We were beginning to become hopeless.

Isabella turned toward me, her legs brushing against my thigh. "I'm scared, Roman," she whispered, brows furrowed together. "I … I like him. My wolf, she loves him, but I don't want to lose you. You're my number one, and you've always been my priority. I'm trying so hard to stay in control and—"

I took her face in my hands and gently stroked my thumbs across her cheek. "You won't lose control."

"But I almost did," she whispered.

"You're not going to lose me if you let him mark you."

She shook her head. "You don't know that. Having him join in the bedroom is fine—*great* even. I know you like being able to dominate both him and me in different ways. It gives you the power that you want and need. But ... a mark is so much different."

I drew my finger across the mark I'd left on Isabella's neck and frowned, my heart aching.

"It's a bond, Roman"—she drew her fingers across the stubble on my face—"a bond that's going to affect me on such a deep level. I don't know how my wolf will react to it or to you once it happens." Tears welled up in her pretty eyes, and she curled her hands around my collar. "I can't lose you. I can't. You're my everything."

After pulling her into my arms, I rocked her back and forth. "I'll do anything for you. I waited years to have you by my side. If you stopped loving me ..." My chest tightened as I thought about it. I would never let Isabella stop loving me. I loved her too fucking much to just give her up.

"I won't," she said, resting her forehead against mine. "I could never stop loving you."

"If you say that and you mean it, then don't worry about him marking you or your wolf wanting to mark him. Forget about that for now. If it happens ... it happens." I bit my tongue because I hated the thought of it happening without me knowing about it. I had been preparing for the worst for weeks now, knowing that this was coming.

Folklore and ancient stories told down the ages said that the two divine wolves had loved each other for eternity and were the strongest wolves to have ever walked this earth. Their bond had survived thousands of years, and it would continue even into our life. I'd expected them to be unable to stay away from each other for weeks now, but what I hadn't expected was for Isabella to stay with me.

I'd thought she'd leave. I'd thought she wouldn't want anything to do with me.

I was wrong.

Isabella stared at me with glossy eyes and then buried her face in the crook of my neck, inhaling deeply and relaxing further. "I just …"

"Don't worry about me," I said before she could continue. Her mind link was racing with thoughts about me instead of where her focus should really lie. "Focus on Dolus and figuring this out. If we can't stop him, then this—*us*—means nothing because there won't be an us anymore. We'll be dead."

When my fingers curled into her sides, she nodded and whimpered softly, as if in agreement. She shifted in my arms so that she straddled my waist on the edge of Vanessa's hospital bed. "I don't know what I'd do without you."

I tugged on a strand of her hair. "You'd still be a cute little ball of power."

"Little?" she asked, arching a brow and giggling. "I'm not little."

"You're smaller than me," I said, grasping her chin and kissing her mouth. "Easy to push around in the bedroom too, if I do say so myself."

She narrowed her eyes. "Is that right, hmm? Okay, well, *Alpha*, I guess you're getting defiant Isabella back next time you get me in bed. No more pushing me around. You're going to have to work for it."

"I work for it every night."

"Do you—"

Isabella's mother knocked on the door and peered into the

room, hands stuffed in her white doctor's coat. "I hope I'm not interrupting anything, but I wanted to inform you that your sister is awake and improving."

After picking Isabella off me, I set her on the ground and took her hand, following her mother out the door and toward my sister's hospital room. Ever since Scarlett or Dolus had taken control of her mind, we had been keeping a close watch over her —my orders. She had woken up in a daze a few times this past week, but she hadn't made much progress—until now.

When we reached Jane's room, she was sitting up in her bed with Raj beside her, staring blankly at the white wall in front of her. Though her eyes had been hazy beyond belief a week ago, they were slowly starting to clear up, and I could finally see her green irises again.

"Jane?" I asked from the door.

She didn't respond.

"Jane, it's me, your brother."

Raj glanced over at me and frowned. "She's not responsive. I've been trying every time she wakes up, but … she's been moving her eyes slightly, and she's stopped mumbling his *and* her name," he said, referring to Dolus and Scarlett. Raj stood and grasped my shoulder. "It's slow, but it's progress. I'll let you spend some time with her alone." He glanced over at Isabella. "Meet me back at the Lycans' packhouse to train tonight. We have some things we need to chat about, and Naomi needs someone to teach her. I can only do so much."

After Isabella nodded, he walked out of the room and shut the door behind him. Isabella ushered me forward to sit in Raj's seat. On the way down, I grasped Jane's hand and wrapped my hand around hers, hoping that the touch of someone familiar would help her remember and retreat back to normal.

She squeezed my hand so slightly that I barely felt it, but it made me smile. She was still in there somewhere, even with Dolus caging her mind and refusing to set her free.

I glanced over my shoulder at Isabella. "If we could find something to speed up her progress, we could apply it to other wolves who might become infected later on."

"We can try, but we first need to find something to heal her. My mom told me that she's tried almost everything to make her better, but nothing has worked. Maybe … maybe Derek has some insight about what happened when he was trapped that could help us." She glanced back at the door and then at her phone. "But I need to go right now. Naomi and the Lycans need me." She kissed me on the lips. "My parents invited you and Kylo over for dinner one night this week. When he comes back, ask him which day works best, and we can go." After another peck on the lips, she hurried to the door. "I'll try to talk to Derek too. I love you."

CHAPTER 6

ISABELLA

"We need to be ready for anything to happen, for one of *us* to be infected," I addressed the Lycans after practice that night, standing in front of the Lycan pack-house and wondering if someone here had already been infected. "We can't take any breaks. We can't let alphas tell us that they don't need our help. We can't lose focus. You are here because you're the strongest warriors from your packs and you want to protect. Don't let opinions rattle you."

My mind flickered to Kylo, who, about a month ago, had hated the idea of Lycans. Now, we were some of the only people who could save our species from Dolus. The Moon Goddess had said it herself.

"Our Moon Goddess is locked away, never to return unless we release her from Dolus's trap. I want everyone working on this project. Nothing comes before this. We must free her, or we will die."

After the group separated, I sighed and walked into the pack-house with Naomi and Raj, unable to focus on much else. Kylo and Roman were still fresh on my mind from earlier, but Roman was right. I couldn't let our relationship get in my way. I had more important things to worry about, like how the hell we were going to release the Moon Goddess from her trap.

I sat at a meeting table and flicked through some papers, glancing up as the door opened, and in walked Oliver, one of the strongest Lycans.

"You wanted to see me?" he asked, glancing between me and Naomi.

"Yes, sit," I said, gesturing to the seat beside Naomi. "I need you to catch Naomi up to speed on everything. Teach her to fight as hard as you do. Teach her to flirt better than any other wolf here. Bring her on missions with you and on routine checkups to the packs up north."

Oliver glanced over at Naomi. "She's, um, a human though."

"Exactly. Even in direct contact with an infected wolf, she didn't contract the corruption. I don't think she will either. She's strong mentally, and she'll be both unstoppable and our greatest strength during this war. Don't let me down."

After Oliver nodded, he gestured for Naomi to follow him through the packhouse and back outdoors to the training field where they'd spar. I glanced out the window to watch them, nodding to myself when they started fighting and Naomi actually began kicking his ass.

"She's going to be a killer."

Raj pushed some papers toward me, drawing me out of my trance. "Twelve packs have been infected so far in the north," Raj said, handing me a list of pack names with a red X beside them or a green check mark. "The names with the check mark refer to the packs who are closer to us, who seem to be resisting the corruption better than the others, though … I'm not sure what's causing it, just like we don't know about Jane."

"When you say resisting corruption, you mean …"

"I mean that the infected are similar to Jane and are in a vegetable-like state, unable to really move or think, but they aren't out of control and killing people like the packs way up north. They're fine and harmless for now."

My lips turned down into a frown. Whole packs were like Jane? Couldn't move? Couldn't think? Couldn't defend themselves against predators or wolves who could kill them without many consequences? If possible, we had to protect them.

"I want them to be brought here," I said to him. "All harmless and corrupted wolves need to be kept safe or else this will be for nothing. Once they are, everything north of our borders will be considered corrupted lands. No civilian goes north after that point, only Lycans."

Raj nodded. "It might take a few days to move everyone, but if we devote resources to it, we could get it done quicker."

"I'll ask Kylo if he's willing to have some wolves help us. I want Roman to stay back though. We've already lost too many people to that corruption. I don't want any more infected until they recover."

Raj sat down and put his hands on his head. "You think Roman will accept that?"

"If I make him," I said with a smile, knowing just how hardheaded Roman really was. After flipping through some more papers, I stopped when I reached some notes about the divine wolves. "What's this?"

Sucking in a breath, Raj took the paper from me and laid it flat on the table. "Since you told me that the Moon Goddess said you and Kylo were the divine wolves, I started to read up on folklore and stories of them in the Lycans' library. It's the only thing that I have been doing while at the hospital with Jane."

"What'd you find?"

"Their story—*your story*—seems very connected to what's happening now, especially with Dolus and corruption. It seems that you and Dolus have met before, in your first lives. There are tons of myths about what happened to you both in your lives, but only one main story about their first lives as the divine wolves, and it's a story with Dolus," Raj said.

I raised a brow. "Well, are you going to tell me, or do I have to find these books and read them myself?"

Raj scratched the back of his head, as if he didn't want to say a word to me about it. Then, he sighed. "Thousands of years ago, Dolus fell in love with a human woman. Wanting to spend eternity with her, Dolus tried endlessly to turn her divine. At this point in the stories, everything seems to get lost in translation, but what I've pieced together is that he wasn't well versed in magic yet, as he was a new god, so he ended up turning her into a divine wolf instead of a divine goddess, and in the process, he turned the leader of her tribe divine too."

My eyes widened at the mere thought of four thousand years ago.

"And because it was done under the full moon, the Moon Goddess claimed these creatures as her own and mated them for eternity, the woman Dolus had once loved gone from him forever. That's why he fights the Moon Goddess and has trapped her—so he can one day have his lover back for himself."

"Me?" I whispered, swallowing hard.

"If the myths are correct, yes. Dolus is after you."

CHAPTER 7

ROMAN

After spending a few hours with Jane and chatting with Isabella's mother about how Jane had improved these past few days, I stood outside the hospital and leaned against the railing that overlooked the forest, staring out into the darkness and wondering where Dolus could be. He had to be lurking, waiting for us to make a mistake, waiting to attack and try to take Isabella away from me.

Wherever that god was ... we had to stop him before he infected more of my pack members. He had already taken Derek and the Moon Goddess, and infected Jane. I didn't know how he had done it and didn't know what was making her better.

Isabella had told me that she'd go visit Derek today to talk about Dolus and try to figure out something, but I hadn't had the heart to tell her that Derek wasn't here. He was just a ghost that Scarlett had left to taunt Isabella forever.

Before Isabella had gone to talk to him earlier this week, I had made sure that touching his ghost wasn't going to do her any harm. I couldn't see him, but I could sense a presence around one of the oak trees. It wasn't dark and evil, just a nagging kind of presence that wouldn't go away.

I hadn't wanted Isabella to hug him and become infected, so I'd tried it before her.

Though I felt that as long as that ghost of Derek remained, he was still alive somewhere in Dolus's hold.

But we had to act fast.

There was no saying that Dolus wouldn't kill Derek.

And there was no way that I'd let him take Isabella from me too.

In the distance, Kylo ran through the woods and shifted to walk into the hospital. I tightened my fists as I stared at him, a growing annoyance in my life. He probably still thought that Isabella was here.

At first, I'd had to fucking like it because the Moon Goddess had chosen this for Isabella.

Hell, I had been fine with it at one point.

Now, after my conversation with Isabella, I slowly started to loathe it because I had seen the way she looked at him earlier. The love in *her* eyes, not her wolf's. She was afraid that she'd pick him over me, and now ... I was terrified of that too.

If I lost her *completely* to Kylo or to Dolus, I would lose control.

Five minutes later, someone slapped me on the back and leaned against the railing with me, dressed in some clothes we kept at the hospital entrance.

Kylo nodded his head back to the hospital back doors. "Where'd Isabella go?"

Instead of looking at the man who was taking my mate—even though I knew it was neither of their faults—I kept my gaze fixed upon the monstrous trees and clenched my jaw. "She went to train with the Lycans. She'll be back for dinner."

"How's your sister?" Kylo asked, sweat from his practice rolling down his neck.

"Fine."

Kylo stayed quiet for a few moments and then pulled his hand off my back. "What's wrong with you?"

"Isabella's parents want you to come to dinner tonight with us. You wanna come?" I asked Kylo, part of me hoping that he'd say no.

They hadn't met before, and I wanted to keep it that way because … I didn't want her parents to like Kylo more than they liked me.

It wasn't that I was jealous of him or possessive of Isabella. Well, maybe a bit possessive. Isabella was and would always be mine, whether Kylo was in the picture or not. But she had her own free will to do whatever she wanted, except when it came to a mate. She couldn't deny Kylo.

That was why I understood.

That was why I tried endlessly every day to accept it.

Did I still resent him a bit? Maybe. Would I rather have Isabella be with me? Fuck yes.

Kylo leaned over the railing next to me and stared out into the forest, his eyes a burning gold, as if his wolf was on the forefront. I clenched my jaw and looked at the ground underneath us, balling my hands into fists.

Though I still had one question.

"Why'd you come to my house this morning, uninvited?" I asked him, tightening my hand, unable to stop myself from feeling nothing but rage building and building and building inside me at the thought of him stepping into my home without either Isabella's or my permission.

Kylo looked over at me, brows furrowed, as if he didn't understand why I was angry. "My wolf felt her calling out to him. She was in heat. I needed to mark her. If your mate was in heat with you, you'd do the same thing, Roman."

"She is my mate," I growled, canines extending past my lips. Something stirred inside me, aching for me to reach forward and snap his neck. Isabella was mine and had always, always, always been mine. She hadn't been with another man. "She's mine."

Kylo placed a hand on my chest. "I'm not going to do anything with her until I tell you."

I shoved my hand into his chest, almost involuntarily. "You were going to mark her."

"What the fuck is wrong with you?" Kylo grabbed me by the collar and held me against him, canines lengthening and his eyes blazing an even brighter gold. "I thought we already talked about her."

Slowly, I pulled my hands away and drew my tongue across my teeth, unsure as to why I had snapped so harshly at him. We'd already talked about it, and I'd already told him that I was fine with it—to an extent. Why had I broken so easily, so quickly too?

"I … I don't know," I said, sucking in a deep breath, my mind reeling with thoughts of … Dolus.

The chaos. The corruption. The sickness.

Had it already infected me? Was that what this was?

I didn't think so because I didn't feel taken or consumed, like Jane. I wasn't off-the-wall crazy and killing people for no reason, like Scarlett and her pack. I could still think and feel and love Isabella. Maybe this wasn't corruption at all, but something else entirely, like an innate need to be with Isabella and always keep her as my own.

CHAPTER 8

ISABELLA

"*Is* Dolus really after me?" I asked Derek, sitting in the field where Scarlett had once threatened to take my life. As it drizzled over the thicket, I ran my fingers through the grass, leaning against a giant oak tree, letting droplets hit my face and run down my cheeks.

After my meeting with the Lycans and listening to the information that Raj had found about Dolus, I felt … uneasy, to say the least. My stomach turned into tight knots at the mere thought of telling Roman about it. I didn't want him to get even more jealous or angry with me, and I especially didn't want him more susceptible to the darkness slithering around the forest.

If he knew *another* man wanted to have me, he'd probably explode into a million pieces.

A raindrop splat against my forehead from a leaf, and I sank down deeper against the tree, vowing that I'd stop this madness before it got worse. We had so much to do that I didn't know we'd be able to fix anything before we were done for.

Derek leaned against the tree beside me and smiled with those dark brown eyes. "I've missed you so much, Isabella."

"Derek …" I rested my head back against the tree bark and groaned internally.

I wanted to crawl over to him, cup his face in my hands, and tell him that he could trust me. After everything he had been through though, I would understand why he couldn't. But I didn't touch him because a week ago, Kylo had told me that he wasn't real.

The Derek facing me now *was* real. He had to be. But I was still nervous.

"You're not helping. Tell me something that you saw when Dolus took you. Anything will do," I complained, pulling grass out of the dirt and watching how easily something alive could die. It had been a simple tug, a simple pull at its roots.

Life was beyond fragile.

"Roman," Derek said, staring through the forest and watching the rain fall.

"What about Roman?"

"Roman." Turning back toward me, he sighed. "He is there."

My brows furrowed together. I couldn't make sense of what he'd said. I sat up and leaned closer to him, narrowing my eyes at his figure that did seem to be a bit blurry around the edges. "What are you talking about?"

Derek pointed deep in the forest. "Roman is there."

Following his finger, I glanced through the forest at Roman's figure as he approached. He stood about a quarter mile north, staring at me in his wolf form and nodding back in the direction of the packhouse. A few moments later, Kylo appeared behind him, his golden eyes blazing as brightly as the sun.

"I have to go," Derek said hastily. "Don't tell Roman that I was here."

As he scurried away, running south into the forest, I frowned at his departing figure and stood. It was almost as if Derek, of all people, was afraid of Roman for some reason. But … if Derek was afraid of Roman, that meant that this Derek wasn't the real one. And that I had been talking to a ghost, one of Dolus's creations.

Deep down, I knew that I always had been … but I missed him so much.

Scarlett had ripped him out of my life, and I … I hadn't been holding up good.

I needed him to talk to, to help deal with all the shit that I had gathered these past few weeks. Because it was difficult, not being able to talk to anyone about anything anymore. I felt bad talking to Roman about Kylo, felt guilty for *talking* to Kylo, and I hadn't been able to chat with Vanessa since she had nearly died.

After pushing my thoughts to the side, I shifted into my wolf and ran toward my mates, ready to have Kylo officially meet my parents for the first time ever. But my parents finally meeting both my mates at once made me nervous because something didn't feel right.

The darkness that had been lurking seemed too close.

CHAPTER 9

KYLO

"*I know the meatloaf is bad, but at least try to finish it for my dad's sake,*" Isabella said to me through the mind link, eyeing the last of the meatloaf on my plate that I'd mashed corn and peas into.

Preparing myself for the worst, I grabbed my last heaping forkful and stuffed it into my mouth, shoving it down my throat and trying hard not to gag on it. Mom would love to come over here and teach her father how to cook. She made shit-tons of food every day for the pack warriors.

"How was the food?" Isabella's father asked.

"Great," Roman said from beside Isabella.

"Best meatloaf I've ever had. We'll have to do it again," I said, which earned me a hard kick under the table from Isabella.

She gave me a pointed stare that told me not to push it and smiled at her father, giving him a thumbs-up—probably because she couldn't lie to his face.

Isabella's mother stood and grabbed some dirty plates to wash in the sink. Roman scooped some from her hands and offered to help. I awkwardly sat next to Isabella because I wanted to help too, but three at one sink would be pushing it.

"So, Isabella tells me that you'll be aiding her in stopping the spread of the corruption," Isabella's father said, leaning back in his seat and looking over at us. "Have you two made any progress? Figured anything else out about Jane?"

Isabella shrugged. "Nothing much yet. Raj is looking into myths about the first divine wolves and Dolus's origin. So far, there's not much, but from what he's told me, this is all for revenge. Dolus seemed like a decent guy before that."

"Decent guy?" Isabella's father and I quipped at the same time.

Isabella opened her mouth to say something else and then pressed her lips together as she sank down further into her seat, as if she had meant to keep that to herself.

Her father chuckled and stood. "Well, I'll let you know if we find anything at the hospital." He shook my hand. "It was nice to finally meet you, Kylo. My shift starts in a half hour, so I'd better go get ready. See you later, Alpha Roman!"

Roman smiled back at him. "See ya."

And I couldn't help but feel a tinge of jealousy over how easily they all got along. Everything seemed so natural for Roman, Isabella, and her parents. I felt like I had been intruding this entire dinner even though they made me as comfortable as could be. Something just felt off about it all. I ached to have that kind of relationship with my mate's parents too.

When her father left, Isabella leaned closer to me. "Did Roman say anything to you?" she whispered, shifting in her seat, blue eyes wide. "My stomach has been in knots since we left the forest."

I glanced over her shoulder at Roman, who smiled at Isabella's mother, and pursed my lips together. I didn't want Isabella to get in the middle of whatever was going on with him. He had gotten way too aggressive today, even after we spoke and agreed upon how we'd approach our relationship.

"No," I said.

Isabella followed my gaze and frowned. "Are you sure?"

"Yes."

She paused and looked back. "Why are you lying to me?"

After blowing out a deep breath, I tilted closer, needing to smell her to calm down because when another alpha was angry, my wolf wanted to come out and match that anger, to protect who I loved.

Though, Isabella moved backward to put space between us.

"I just ... I don't want you to hate him." I sighed. And I might want to keep this relationship with Isabella going strong.

My wolf had become so much more possessive over her these past few days, especially after she started her heat. If we went backward instead of forward in our relationship, I feared that he'd lose control.

She rolled her eyes. "Come on. I can't hate Roman."

But she could hate me. She could refuse to be with me because of his insecurities.

"Have you noticed anything different about Roman? Does he seem more aggressive since he came home from the forest with Scarlett?" I asked her.

"Not really. Why?" She furrowed her brows at me. "I mean, I honestly wouldn't notice if he was more aggressive. I love him that way and wouldn't complain. But overall, he hasn't seemed that way."

"We talked earlier," I said. "He seemed different—that's all."

"In what kind of way?" she asked.

I wanted to tell her, but I didn't. It was wrong to hide it, yet I couldn't help myself. I wanted to be with Isabella even if Roman was in the picture. I would deal with it any way that I could, but if Isabella told me that we needed to stop seeing each other ...

Fuck, I didn't know what I'd do.

I fucking loved her.

After arching another hard brow, she pushed me to the kitchen. "Well, until you figure it out, why don't you and Roman go clear the air? Go help him with the dishes and tell my mom to come over here. I need to talk to her."

Shoving my hands into my pockets, I dismissed Isabella's mom and grabbed a plate from the sink to wash it alongside Roman. Roman grabbed the plate from me and swiped a rag over it to dry it.

"Listen, I'm sorry," Roman said, frowning at Isabella in the other room, talking to her mom. "I … I don't know what got into me earlier. I lost control. It won't happen again."

"Do you lose control often?" I asked him, clenching my jaw.

Roman tensed and looked over at me. "What's that supposed to mean?"

"It's just a question." I grabbed another plate.

"You said it like you were accusing me of something." Roman snatched the plate from me and glided the rag against this one, setting it atop the other dried plates. "You're not one to talk. You lost control this morning and ended up in my house without my permission."

"You never told us what happened with Scarlett," I said, staying cautious and clear-minded because someone needed to.

Roman was Isabella's mate, so I didn't blame her for not thinking anything was wrong with him. But he wasn't mine, and I had seen right through his lies since we were teenagers.

Yet at the same time, I couldn't really think clearly. My wolf had been responding to Isabella's, needing to please her as soon as humanly possible, aching to mark what was his, becoming more aggressive by the day until he had his fill of her.

My point of view was murky at the moment.

"Why do you want to know about Scarlett?" Roman asked me.

"Because you disappeared for over a day with her."

"And I brought her back, just as we'd planned. She wasn't going to willingly come back to your pack with you. She doesn't fucking like you." Roman blew out a deep breath, his fists relaxing. "Look, I did what I needed to do to get her back here."

"Did you have sex with her?" I asked, gritting my teeth. "Because you haven't said how."

Roman snarled, "What kind of stupid question is that? I would never break Isabella's trust. I would never sleep with another woman. I have fucking loved her from the moment I turned eighteen, and I completely dumped Scarlett because I knew Isabella was my mate. Don't fucking ask shit like that. It makes you seem jealous."

"Over Isabella?" I asked, arching a brow. "Because you know where I stand with her and you."

"Over Scarlett," Roman said, nostrils flared. "And if we're asking each other stupid questions, I have one for you."

"Go ahead," I said, feeling like nothing could stop me.

Roman paused, as if he didn't want to ask, but he wasn't in control right now. His wolf was. "How does it feel not to have been chosen as true mates with Isabella in this lifetime, knowing that you were chosen to be together for thousands of years before now but that I am her first mate in this time around?"

I balled my hands into fists. "You want my real answer or a respectful one?"

"Your real answer."

"It fucking sucks," I said, watching Isabella hug her mother. "I want her to myself. If I had it my way, I wouldn't be sharing her with you. If the Moon Goddess had made us mates, then I wouldn't have to worry." Knowing that I wasn't going to get anywhere, arguing with him like this—though I was the one to start it—I sighed and relaxed under Isabella's intense stare from the living room. "But it is what it is now. You were my best friend. I guess I'd rather ... have her be with you than someone I hated."

Seething, Roman glanced over at me, his fists unraveling and his anger slowly subsiding.

I blew out another deep breath. "Did you at least see anything unusual while you were with Scarlett? Anything we could use to take her and Dolus down?"

Roman paused, gaze faltering for the briefest moment, and then he finally said, "Her pack was vacant. Completely vacant, except some dead bodies. The rumors about war breaking out are true. Her pack members are destroying people out there."

CHAPTER 10

ISABELLA

*L*ater that night, I lay on my back with Roman over me, his cock buried deep in my pussy.

"Roman," I whispered, digging my claws into his back and panting. "My heat."

It was four a.m., and I hadn't fallen asleep all night because I feared that if I did, my wolf would take control of me and force me to run to Kylo's without my knowledge. So, Roman stayed up with me all night, not falling asleep once. And when I'd finally felt that first singe of the fire inside me, he'd rolled me onto my back and told me that he'd take me for as long as I needed him to.

Roman growled into my ear, his canines brushing against his mark and making me shiver in delight. "It's worse than last time." He drew his nose up the side of my neck and grabbed my throat, squeezing it lightly. "Do you want Kylo?"

Knowing that he didn't feel comfortable yet, I shook my head. If I had to endure heat for the rest of my damn life before Roman felt comfortable, then I would. Kylo might've been my first mate ever, the other half of my divine wolf, but he wasn't my mate in this lifetime. I shouldn't be having these thoughts and this reaction to Kylo.

The Moon Goddess had even admitted that we weren't mates.

If she'd wanted us to be, then we would've been. But she had given Kylo the option of having another mate, and he'd declined. This had to be her doing, wanting Kylo and I to be together even though she knew that I had a mate. As much as I needed and wanted to save her, I was kind of annoyed with her for doing this to Kylo, Roman, and me.

And for what? All to dispose of Dolus? If those myths were based on fact, then the Moon Goddess had taken me—or the first divine wolf—away from Dolus. She had caused this chaos to go off throughout the world because she wanted the wolves to worship her.

Don't get me wrong. I loved—*loved?*—Kylo too. But I loved Roman first.

With my skin in flames, I felt my wolf awakening. I sniffed the air and smelled Kylo in the distance. Everything inside my wolf relaxed, knowing that he was coming to get her. But I was slowly starting to despise her.

Before I knew it, Kylo ripped the bedroom door open and stormed into the room, his eyes golden as the sun. He hurried over to us, canines lengthened, completely controlled by his wolf. I could see it in his eyes that this wasn't the real him.

Just as he was about to pounce on me, Roman shot his arm back and grabbed him by the throat, stopping him instantly. My eyes widened, my pussy clenching around Roman at his strength. Roman had never been stronger than Kylo, especially when he was controlled by his human and Kylo was controlled by his wolf. Wolves usually overpowered humans easily.

But this was … dominance.

"Fuck me harder," I whispered, closing my burning eyes and relaxing only slightly against the mattress at the smell of Kylo and the way Roman's mouth glided all over my body. "Please, Roman, harder."

Roman shoved Kylo back so hard that he slammed into the

wall and left a damn indent, and then he hovered over me—his large body shielding mine—and thrust into my pussy over and over. Trapping me in, he made my body feel like it was scorching with the sweat dripping down my neck and the fire blazing in my core.

I dug my trembling fingers into his back, hard enough to draw blood, and howled to the Moon Goddess. Why had she put me through a second heat, even after I mated Roman? It was a terrible thing to do to one of her strongest warrior wolves who had vowed to fight for her.

Desperate to ease the pain, I pressed my lips to Roman's and pleaded with him to continue. I pulled away slightly to glance over at Kylo, who was about to really lose control this time and transform into his wolf. And something about Roman not giving a single fuck and continuing to fuck me while a threat loomed in our own bedroom was wild and made me clench even harder.

"Your tight little pussy is mine, Isabella," Roman growled into my ear, sucking and gnawing on his mark, cooling me down slightly, though my wolf begged for me to push him away and run into Kylo's arms. Roman lifted his head, grabbed my jaw, and forced me to look up at him. "You're fucking mine. You'll look at me when *my cock* makes you come. Do you fucking understand me?"

"But Kylo is—"

"I don't give a fuck about Kylo losing control in our bedroom," Roman growled, grasping Kylo by the neck again when he lunged at us and shoving him away. "You're fucking mine. He can try to rip me to pieces to get a taste of you tonight, but it's not happening."

My pussy tightened around his cock, my legs trembling as I caught the sight of Roman.

Roman rammed himself into me one more time and captured one of my nipples in his mouth, tugging on it roughly. "The way your sopping pussy clenches on me tells me that you fucking love it too."

Sweat rolling down my chest, I tugged up on his hair and arched my back. My body both felt like it was on fire and was fucking shivering in pleasure at the same time. I rode out his thrusts, bucking my hips back and forth, needing a release.

"Beg for it," Roman scolded, pulling out of me and flipping me around until I lay on my stomach. He wrapped his hand under my throat and leaned his entire weight on my back, so I really couldn't move if I tried. "Fucking look at your mate over there and tell him that you want *me* to make you come."

Staring over at Kylo, who bared his large canines at Roman, I moaned. "Please, Roman," I whimpered, panting. The room seemed to get even hotter, the closer I came to my orgasm. "Please, give it to me. Make me come for you. I need it."

One last time, Kylo lunged at us, and I reactively squeezed my eyes closed. But as the moments passed, I opened them back up to see that Roman had grabbed him by the throat, kept him staggered in the air inches from us, and rammed his cock into me one more time, making me come. I clawed into my pillow, ripping it at its seams and screaming Roman's name to the high heavens, my entire body trembling as an unruly orgasm tore through my body.

CHAPTER 11

ISABELLA

I lay back on the bed, my heat slowly subsiding but still lingering at the forefront. It had been worse than last time, and I could only imagine how the following nights would be for both me and Kylo if I didn't let him mark me. My wolf wanted him so bad, but deep down, I truthfully didn't want it. Not only did I want to wait until Roman was ready, but *I* wanted to be ready too.

And right now, I wasn't.

What I had with Roman was really fucking good. I didn't want to fuck it up.

"Get out of my house," Roman growled at Kylo.

Placing a hand on his chest, I calmed him down only slightly. "No, we need to talk about this because I can't do this another night, and we're no fucking closer to fixing this whole thing. We need to figure us out because Dolus is getting closer."

After grumbling to himself, Roman turned to Kylo. "If you fucking touch her, I'll kill you."

After cutting my gaze at Roman, he leaned against the headboard, hand on my shoulder.

I looked back at Kylo. "It's not that I don't want you because my wolf does. It's just …"

"Just what?" Kylo asked, voice quieter than I had ever heard it.

"Kylo," I whispered, taking his hand in mine despite Roman growling. "My wolf wants you to mark me, but I … I don't want it right now. I know it sucks. I know it's going to be hard. But I … I feel like we barely know each other. And while I feel connected to you through my wolf, I need something a bit more than … this."

As soon as the words left my mouth, I pressed my lips together and looked down between us, my chest tightening. I'd hated saying it so freaking much, but it'd needed to be said. Roman and I had spent our entire lives together. I had known him since I was a kid. I had barely known Kylo for a few weeks.

And why the hell was the heat happening now? Had the Moon Goddess wanted us to be mates so badly that she created a bond between our wolves to override the bond between Roman and me? I had only known of wolves who went through heat once, not twice, unless a new bond formed.

"If we're truly the divine wolves and we have a bond in every life despite the Moon Goddess, then why didn't I feel the heat as soon as I met you and my wolf recognized you? Why didn't it happen during the nights we spent with the other Wolf Moon wolves?"

"Maybe the Moon Goddess set forth another bond between us," Kylo said. "She had to have a reason for wanting us together. She wouldn't put you through heat for nothing. Maybe this is the way to defeat Dolus."

My stomach tightened at the information I had learned earlier with Raj. I hadn't told either of them yet, but I needed to get it out because while wolves only looked up to the Moon Goddess, it might not have always been that way, if the myths were correct.

Don't get me wrong. I still wanted to save her. But when she'd created this extra bond between Kylo and me, she might not have been looking out for the species, more focused on keeping her control.

"There's something I need to tell you about the beginning of … us." I gnawed on the inside of my cheek and scooted closer to both of them, my thighs over Roman's and my hands still on Kylo. My throat dried at the thought of bringing this up in front of Roman too, because he was already stressed out about Kylo, and now, he'd be stressed about Dolus too.

"What is it?" Roman asked, tucking a strand of hair behind my ear.

I glanced over at him through wide eyes. "Please, don't hate me for it."

"I could never hate you, Isabella," Roman said with a slight smile, though I could tell that he was preparing himself for the worst of the absolute worst. And I hated seeing that in those green eyes of his, the pain and anguish just waiting to be unleashed.

Instead of squeezing Kylo's hand, I found myself moving closer to Roman because it'd calm him down. I gripped his hand and furrowed my brows. "Raj told me earlier that Dolus is after *me*, that my wolf was his first … *love*, I guess."

Roman tensed, canines lengthening. "You're fucking kidding me, right, Isabella?"

Biting down on my lip, I shook my head and embraced his hand even tighter with my own. "Let me continue, Roman. You're going to want to hear this." After blowing out a deep breath, I told him about how the Moon Goddess had wanted followers so she mated Kylo and me and that Dolus and I had actually been in love.

Well, not me, but *my wolf.*

I was not in love with Dolus, and I could never be in love with Dolus.

It was my wolf who had been driving me crazy, my wolf who

had mated Kylo, my wolf who had once loved Dolus too. Not me, and I really, really, really wanted Roman to see that. My wolf and I lived in the same body, but my human soul belonged to Roman. Nobody else's now.

And oddly enough, the more I talked about Dolus, the quieter both Kylo and Roman became.

Kylo rubbed a hand over his face and grunted. "This is why he's doing what he's doing—why he took the Moon Goddess and why he keeps hurting people close to you, Isabella. I can't believe there's someone else. This is even more reason to let me mark you sooner rather than later. We're stronger together."

"Did you not just hear anything that Isabella said?" Roman snapped, a growl rumbling from his chest. "The Moon Goddess paired you and Isabella together because Dolus had turned you into divines, not because it was her doing. She wanted you together to worship *her*."

Kylo growled, canines lengthening, "Sounds like you're defending Dolus."

"Sounds like *you're* trying to coerce Isabella into mating with you when she already said that she didn't want to at the moment."

Nails lengthening into claws, Kylo leaned closer, moments away from shifting into his wolf and trying to rip Roman apart. Roman attempted to pull me behind him, but I refused to move. We were supposed to be talking to fix this, not to make it even more of a mess.

"You're selfish," Kylo barked at Roman.

"*You're* the one being selfish," Roman retorted. "Isabella said she doesn't want to do it. Don't push her. She makes her own decisions and always fucking has. She's not going to mate you and listen to *your* orders."

Placing a hand on either of their chests, I held them apart and cursed because they both had solid points to their arguments, but I wasn't going to let either of them make my decisions for me. I pushed them away from each other. "Stop it! Stop it now! We have a war that we need to fucking win. I can't be dealing with you two constantly fighting."

When they growled at each other, I shook my head and stormed out of bed, throwing on some clothes and grabbing my backpack. "I'm not dealing with this right now. Figure this out yourself because, obviously, with me, it's not fucking working. I'm going to the Lycans' packhouse to start for the day. Don't call me unless you two are civil."

"Isabella—"

"No, Kylo," I snapped. "Work it the fuck out. I'm leaving."

And before I could stop myself, I ran out of the room and into the forest, pushing myself as quickly as I could toward the Lycans and wondering if those men would ever be on good terms with each other. I'd thought that we were making solid progress, but it seemed that the past couple days, we'd taken a huge step backward. And I didn't know why or how it had happened, but I needed to find out.

CHAPTER 12

ISABELLA

"You look tired," Raj said, rocking back and forth on his heels in the forest.

"Gee, thanks," I said, staring at the Lycans training and yawning. My eyes felt so heavy, my mind foggy with thoughts about Kylo and Roman, my muscles so tired from enduring the heat last night. All I wanted to do was crawl back up into bed with Roman and fall asleep in his arms, but I needed him and Kylo to figure out whatever was going on between them. Now.

"Late night?"

"Early morning," I said to him. "I had my heat again."

Raj tensed and looked over. "Again? For Kylo? Why now?"

I shrugged my shoulders and wanted to curse the Moon Goddess out loud. I didn't know why she'd decided to give me heat for a second time and for someone who had only been my mate in past lives. I was already mated to Roman.

"If I knew, I'd tell you. But, fuck, I don't know how much longer I can endure it." I swiped a hand across my face and then directed the Lycans to switch partners. "Can you look more into the folklore behind this? I need to understand why the Moon Goddess did what she did and more about Dolus."

"Anything you need," Raj said, glancing down at his watch. "Do you think you'll be awake enough to start transporting people from the northern packs? You can stay and rest here, if you'd like. I can oversee it. We're just taking people from the closest pack today to see how easily and smoothly it will go."

Staring out into the crowd of Lycans, I shook my head and watched Naomi. Naomi tossed one over her hip, the movement looking so smooth. My lips curled into a smile at how easily she had adjusted to life as a Lycan. We had been training her endlessly, and yet she continued to keep up with the rest of us. A true Lycan herself.

"Yes, and I'll accompany Naomi. I want to chat with her," I said.

After nodding, Raj whistled to signal the end of practice. "Get into two teams. We'll be transporting the first northern pack past our borders to protect them from the warring packs and the corruption. One team will be taking cars because many of these people are currently in a vegetable-like state and won't be simply transported through the woods. The other team will run there to prepare the woods and their pack for transportation."

Once everyone started to disperse, I nodded to Raj. "You take the cars. I'll go with the others." I glanced back at the Lycans and headed toward the woods. "Naomi and Oliver's team, come with me. We're running."

Twenty minutes later, we stood at the closest northern pack and shifted. It seemed desolate, not many people walking around and even fewer shops open. I gnawed on the inside of my cheek and prepared as many people as I could for transportation to pass the Lycan borders.

"There are so many people who are … barely there," Naomi whispered once Raj arrived and started placing the people inside cars, strapping them in. "They remind me of my mom."

"Your mom?" I asked, the wind blowing hair into my face.

Naomi frowned. "My dad cheated on my mom a while ago with someone from a northern pack. When she found out, she was so devastated that ... that she refused to leave the house and had no will to live anymore," she whispered.

My eyes widened. "Oh my gosh, I'm so sorry."

After shaking her head, Naomi gave me a smile. "Don't be sorry. It happened. There's nothing I can do to switch it back, but it gave me a reason to start training. I wanted to kill the woman who had taken my dad from our family, but ... I'm glad I didn't. If I had, I wouldn't be here with you, doing something that most *wolves* only dream of."

Tugging her in closer to me, I rested my head on her shoulder and smiled. "I'm glad you're here too. Most northern packs, especially now, are corrupt like that. They always have been. If you want, I will look into their pack for you and see what I can do. I know nothing can bring your family back together, but maybe it will give you a sense of peace."

With wavering eyes and a slightly trembling smile, Naomi nodded. "I would like that, but ... only when you have time. I have a couple of questions that I've always wanted to ask that woman who destroyed my sister's and my childhood." Naomi looked back at the transportees. "But work before pleasure. I should get back to helping."

I crossed my arms and watched her disappear into a house.

Oliver walked up to my side and smiled. "She's really powerful. I'm glad that you paired me with her. She's actually pushing me to become smarter and stronger."

"As she should be," I said to him with a smile, seeing that excited look in his eyes. I arched a brow at him. "Is she your mate?"

He chuckled. "I wish because she's amazing. Whoever ends up being mates or married to her, whether wolf or human, they'll be so damn lucky."

CHAPTER 13

ROMAN

"*I*sabella wants us to talk, so let's talk," Kylo said to me.

While I wanted Isabella to be happy, I didn't want to talk to him anymore today. I was checked the fuck out and didn't want to have another endless conversation with him. It sickened me that he couldn't take no for a fucking answer.

A couple weeks ago, he had told me to grow up and be the man Isabella needed me to be. Now that I was, now that I had found the strength to protect her, he thought *he* could be the one to walk all over her. It was fucking wrong.

After tugging on a shirt, I found myself walking away from the conversation and out my bedroom door to head for my office. I contacted Cayden and told him to meet me there because I had a job that I desperately needed done.

Kylo followed me and grabbed my shoulder, pulling me back. "Are you going to tell me what's up with you?" Kylo asked, golden eyes of his wolf still prominent. "Because you've been acting awfully suspicious lately, and it's not fucking looking good for you."

I shoved his hand off me and growled, "I don't have anything to hide. I just don't want to fight with you again. I'm tired of it, Kylo. Isabella is tired of it. Drop it and go back home, where you belong. When Isabella is ready, she'll let you fucking know."

Though, now, I didn't want Isabella to ever be ready to mate someone like him.

"Her wolf is ready," Kylo said to me. "She calls out for me every night."

"Her wolf is ready, but she isn't!" I shouted at him, continuing to the office. "Don't you understand that? When you mate someone, you mate both the wolf and the human. You don't get to pick and choose. If you can't respect her wishes, leave. Don't come back until you can."

Instead of leaving me alone, like I fucking wanted him to, he kept pushing. "Did you let Dolus get to you?" Kylo asked me, lips curled in an ugly snarl. "Is that why you can't tell either of us about what happened when you went to get Scarlett? Did you let him corrupt you, like he did your sister?"

An unruly growl ripped out of my throat, and I shoved him back. "What's your fucking problem? Why can't you fucking leave it alone? I brought her back for us. I don't want to fucking relive seeing all those people dead and taken by the corruption. Fucking stop it."

We glared at each other for a few moments until Kylo nodded. "If that's what you want to believe, fine. Believe it. But I'm going to find out the fucking truth. I'm not going to let Isabella blindly believe you because *you* met her first and before me."

Rubbing a hand across my face, I let out a breath. "Get off my fucking property before I make you."

After another couple moments, Kylo growled and ran off until I couldn't see him through the woods anymore. I cursed at him and met Cayden in my office. I shut the door behind me and locked it, so nobody would think about interrupting.

"Don't tell Isabella," I said to Cayden, sitting.

I blew out a deep breath at the thought of going behind her

back, but I didn't trust that man not to hurt her or try to come between us. We had given him a chance, and he had continuously forced himself upon Isabella. I would not let Isabella feel the way that Ryker must've made his mate feel when he marked her and got her pregnant.

"She's the luna and leader of the Lycans," Cayden said hesitantly.

"And she's my mate too. I need to protect her." I narrowed my gaze. "Promise me that you won't tell her about what I'm about to ask you to do."

After swallowing hard, Cayden nodded. "I promise I won't tell her."

Glancing out my office window and into the dark morning forest, I sighed. "I don't trust Kylo, not anymore. I need you to keep an eye on him and make sure he doesn't try to come close to Isabella while I'm not around."

"Roman, you're asking me to watch Isabella's wolf's mate?"

I growled, "Isabella is *my* mate."

Cayden grunted and blew out a deep breath, standing up and walking to the door. "Fine. I'll get someone to do it, and I won't tell Isabella about it, but you should. She's going to find out and get angry with you again for going behind her back. And who knows? Maybe this time, she'll have had enough of it."

Unable to hold myself back, I stood at lightning speed, stormed over to him, and pinned him against the wall with my hand around his throat. "Isabella won't find out, and if she does, she won't leave me." She couldn't. "I'm doing this for her well-being. She has other things to worry about."

Cayden nodded. "I don't want you to get hurt. You're the only person keeping this pack together, and you have been since your parents died. If Dolus gets to you, all of us will be soon to go too. I can't let that happen."

Releasing his throat, I took a step back and let my fists unravel. "Nothing will happen."

Dolus wouldn't get to me—at least, he couldn't because I refused to let it happen. It would break Isabella into pieces. But Kylo had been accusing me that Dolus already had, and I had been already growing more aggressive by the day. I feared that he was already here.

CHAPTER 14

KYLO

*R*oman had told me not to come back until I could respect Isabella's wishes, but he didn't feel that pull with her wolf that I had every fucking night lately. Neither he nor she respected her wolf's wishes. For nights, I'd been holding myself back from claiming her aching wolf, who was mine, who I should've claimed already, who wanted *me*.

I didn't know how much longer I would be able to hold back.

We needed each other more than Isabella could even understand.

And if Roman and Isabella couldn't see that, then I needed to wait a bit longer, needed to hold out to prove to her that Roman wasn't the man she should be with. No matter how shitty it was, I had to do this for us.

"We need our mate," my wolf growled inside my mind.

After balling my hands into fists, I continued to run in my human form through the forest, knowing that if I did give him control, he'd lead me to Isabella or to Roman to kill him. It wasn't that I hated Roman, but lately, I'd just had the fucking urge to rip his head off his body and serve it to Isabella on a platter.

He wasn't good for her. I was. I had always thought that, and I always would.

"*Find mate. Mark mate. Claim mate.*"

Sucking in a breath, I saw my packhouse from a distance and continued toward it. "*You know we can't do that. We have to respect her wishes not to be marked by us yet. She'll come around.*"

"*Not when Roman is talking into her ear about us.*"

"*This is Isabella's decision.*"

More possessive than usual, my wolf growled at me, "*No, this is Roman's decision. A bad fucking decision, and you know it. You're not going to let him have her after everything we've been through with Isabella. You love her. I love her. Don't let him take her from us.*"

I ran up to my warriors, who walked around my prison in the forest. "You're dismissed," I said to them, grabbing a key from my main guard and pushing it into the door to unlock it. Glancing over my shoulder, I made sure that all were gone before I entered the prison and dead-bolted the door behind me.

With all the corruption going on around these parts, I needed to make sure that nobody had access to or even *knew* about the cells underneath the prison. Who knew which of my prisoners were corrupted? I sure as hell didn't, but I didn't doubt that someone knew something. And I couldn't risk my prisoner escaping.

After walking to a back hallway, I found the hatch to the lower cells, opened it up, and jumped down into the underground cells. Lighting a torch with a spare match from my pocket, I let the flames guide me through a tunnel of stone walls and to a second hallway of cells. Inside the last cell was my prisoner, who I needed so desperately to give me the ingredients that had created the flower that could kill Wolf Moon warriors.

I needed to figure out how to reverse the effects in case it fell into the wrong hands. Isabella and I were both susceptible to be killed by it, and I couldn't let that happen. Not after all the shit I had done to get here.

Placing the torch in a stand, I crossed my arms and stood in front of the woman. "Is the flower lethal to just wolves born under the Second Wolf Moon?"

She refused to make eye contact with me and looked at the dirty concrete floor. "I don't know what you're talking about. Won't you let me go? I've answered all your questions and done everything you needed me to do. Just let me go."

"I need answers."

"I. Don't. Know."

"Give me a greater response than that. You know botany better than anyone."

I leaned down and opened the case that the flower sat in. The Moon Goddess had said that I would need to use it to save the species, but I needed to know if I could use it on the corrupted or if I could use it on Roman if I had to—because Roman couldn't open his damn mouth about what had happened when he found Scarlett, and I wouldn't let him have Isabella for the rest of our lives alone. She was mine.

"Will it kill Roman?" I asked her.

She stared up at me. "Why do you want to kill Roman?"

"You know why. He's corrupted."

"He's not, and you know it."

"Isabella is resisting the mate bond," I said to her.

She flared her nostrils. "That's why you're going to kill her mate?! Listen, Kylo, you need to let Isabella go for once and for all. I have done everything that you've asked. Every. Last. Thing. Even shit that I vowed never to do again for you in any lifetime. I have better things, more divine things to do than being locked in a cell."

"Don't worry, *A*. I'm not going to kill Roman."

At least, not until I exposed him for being the corrupt man he was. I would not let Roman lead Isabella into the darkness with him. Now that the Moon Goddess had forged a bond between us, Isabella was mine to protect, mine to love, mine to be with forever and ever and ever, in every life.

CHAPTER 15

ISABELLA

"*A*re you going home tonight?" Raj asked, leaning against my doorframe and yawning. He wiped his tired eyes and sighed. "It's almost one a.m. Roman probably has the whole pack out in the forest by now, trying to find you."

I stared out into the forest through the large windows in my office, my eyes desperately wanting to close and get some rest for the night. We'd had such a long day, transporting all the corrupted people who couldn't quite move themselves. All I wanted to do was sleep, but I didn't trust my wolf anymore.

Every time I slept, I always woke up in a fit of heat, aching for Kylo.

That wasn't happening again. Not until I was ready. *If* I would ever be ready.

"I'm gonna stay here for a bit longer," I said, nodding to the files on my desk that didn't really have anything inside of them. I'd just put them there to trick my brain into thinking that I actually had loads of work to do. But my brain wasn't as dumb as I'd hoped it would be.

Instead of departing and heading back to Jane, Raj walked into the room and collapsed onto the chair in front of me, leaning forward on his forearms and giving me that look he always did when he knew something was up. "What is it?"

Gliding a hand across my face, I blew out a deep breath and sighed. "Nothing."

"Roman?"

"No."

"Kylo?"

I stayed quiet.

"Is it the mating problem that you were telling me about?" Raj asked, yawning again.

Feeling so damn defeated because I seemed to have no control over myself anymore, I slumped my shoulders forward, pulled my knees to my chest, and cradled myself in the middle of the Lycans' packhouse. "It's so stupid. My wolf does whatever the hell she wants, and I have no control over her. I've always had control over her and her brattiness. Now, with Kylo … I have none."

Raj stayed quiet for a moment. "You don't want him to mark you?"

"Not now," I said, shaking my head. "We have too much going on."

"Do you love him?" Raj started. "Or do you love the idea of him? An alpha who would let you do as you want, who respected you from the beginning and gave you the power, who tells you that he will wait for you but then can't control his wolf for long enough?"

After letting out a long sigh, I shrugged. I had no freaking idea how I felt about him.

My wolf, on the other hand …

"If Roman and Kylo were both corrupted and you had the power to only save one, who would you save and spend the rest of your life with?" he asked me, the moonlight glimmering against his tan face. "Roman or Kylo?"

"Kylo," my wolf whispered in my mind, slowly awakening. And

when she woke up in the middle of the night, that meant one thing: the heat would be here soon.

I fucking hated the damn heat so much.

"My wolf would choose Kylo," I said, gnawing on my cheek. "I wouldn't."

"Would she leave you if you chose to save Roman?" Raj asked.

I waited for her response, knowing that she was listening to every single word that we said. Would she leave me if I chose to be with Roman and nobody else for the rest of this life? She had hundreds of other lives she could spend with Kylo. This was my only one with Roman. Hell, this was really my only one too.

My wolf and I might be the same person, but I didn't remember all those past lives. My wolf seemed like she did, but me? No way. All I remembered was this one, and that was why I would choose Roman if I had to make the decision to save one or the other. I didn't know Kylo as much as I knew Roman, and I didn't love Kylo as much either. If truly at all.

Her response never came.

So, I answered for her.

"No, my wolf wouldn't leave me. And even if she would, I would still choose Roman."

Raj cracked a small smile and stood. "Then, why don't you reject Kylo?"

Finally deciding to come alive inside of me, my wolf growled, *"No. Can't reject mate."*

I seized control of her, gripped the chair armrests until my knuckles turned white, and sat up straight, urging Raj to continue while my wolf snarled, barked, and howled inside of me, demanding that I stop listening right this second.

"We will never reject our mate!" she scolded. *"He's the only one who understands us."*

"You need to focus, and this drama is really taking your mind off things. You're tired and upset and too tied up with Roman and Kylo to think straight. Your wolf is probably begging you not to, but please consider it. We need you to defeat Dolus," Raj said.

"No! Mate with him, not reject."

And while I wanted to say I had it in me to reject him right here and right now, I didn't. These past few weeks had completely exhausted me to no end. If my wolf left at this exact moment, I would be even more vulnerable to corruption.

"Whatever you decide, you know I'm here for you." Raj gave me a half-smile and then nodded toward a manila envelope on the corner of my desk. "Oh, and, uh, because I know you won't be heading home anytime soon, I found some more information about Dolus, the first divine wolves, and the Moon Goddess. You might want to check it out."

Grabbing for the envelope, I smiled back at him. "I appreciate you."

After he left, I sank down in my seat, kicked my legs up onto the desk, and opened the file, all the while ignoring my wolf, who was still going berserk inside my mind. And just as I was about to fall into a night of reading, someone opened my door and walked into my office with a sinful smirk on his face and glowing golden eyes.

"Isabella."

CHAPTER 16

ISABELLA

"*D*on't let me stop you," Roman said, stalking around my desk and gently squeezing my shoulders. "My Isabella is such a hard worker that she forgot to call me to say that she was going to be home a little late."

I placed the papers down on my desk and glanced back. "I'm sorry. Are you mad?"

He growled playfully, burying his face into the crook of my neck and grazing his teeth against my soft spot and his mark. I shivered in delight, my nipples hardening and warmth gathering between my legs.

"No," he said, sprawling a large hand across my stomach and moving his fingers into my pants to rub my clit in small, torturous circles. He grasped a fistful of my hair and pulled it back, so I stared right up into those devilish golden eyes. "But from now on, I want to know where my mate is at one a.m., especially with the corruption. Understand?"

My lips curled up into a smirk. "And if I don't tell you?"

"Do you want to find out what will happen?"

"Maybe …"

In a moment, he whirled my chair around, grabbed my hips,

and pulled my ass to the edge of the seat, kneeling and pulling down my pants. A rush of heat ran to my core, my pussy clenching as I caught the sight and the feel of Roman's large canines trailing up the insides of my thighs.

Before I could stop him, he buried his face between my legs, held my thighs apart, and flicked his tongue against my clit, hitting me exactly where I liked it. I moaned loudly, the pleasure rushing to my core. He pressed his mouth to my folds, kissing and licking down to my entrance, and then he shoved two large fingers into me and pumped them in and out.

My body jerked, my breasts bouncing, nipples pressing hard against my shirt. I thrust my hand into his hair to hold him steady, my hips bucking against his hot mouth. He stared up at me with those dark golden eyes that shimmered under the moonlight, resting his hands under my thighs and spreading my legs even wider.

He flicked his tongue over and over against my clit, making me clench even harder. "Mine," he said, thrusting his fingers into my pussy.

I squirmed in his hold and tried to pull my knees together, feeling the pressure rise in my core. His fingers moved in and out of me, his stubble tickling my thighs.

When I threw my head back and moaned out loud, Roman grabbed my jaw and forced me to look down at him. "Do you want pups, Isabella?"

My eyes widened, pussy tightening around his fingers. *Pups?*

"Your pussy got so tight for me. Let's make it even tighter." He added a third finger and flicked his tongue against my clit again. "Now, answer me. Do you want pups with me?"

Again, I clenched on him, which should've been a damn answer in itself, but Roman wouldn't accept it. He wanted to hear me say that I had been dreaming of having his pups since *before* I knew that he was my mate. But now … wasn't the best time.

"Roman, I—"

He gently sucked my clit between his lips and tugged. "Yes. Or. No."

I swallowed hard and nodded. "Yes," I whispered.

"Good." Roman stood between my legs and undid his zipper. "Because I'm going to put a baby in you tonight. I'm not waiting any longer. I want little yous running around the packhouse to keep me company while you're here, doing what you do best."

My pussy tightened even more as he slid the head of his cock into me. Inch by inch, he thrust into me slowly until he was buried in my tight hole. He groped my breasts, squeezing them hard in his hands, and pulled me toward him with each thrust.

I dug my nails into his taut chest, trying to keep my breathing even, but with every thrust, he drove me closer to the edge.

"Please, give me one," I begged, knowing that it would get him off and make him harder. "I've wanted your pups for so damn long, Roman."

He grazed his canines against my shoulder and bit down hard enough to draw blood. I moaned louder as his cock pumped harder into me, the pressure rising quickly in my core. Who knew begging Roman to give me pups would … make me feel so good?

Though my wolf was quiet.

"More," I whispered. "Give me more."

He trailed his nose up the side of my neck, grasped my hips, and stood up taller, pounding away at my insides. I gripped the armrests, my knuckles white. He spit on his fingers and rubbed them into my clit in small circles, his thrusts long and slow, hitting my G-spot every time.

So close. I was so … fucking … close …

When his fingers moved even faster, I parted my lips and screamed out his name, feeling him come inside of me. Wave after wave of pleasure rushed through my body, my toes numb.

I let him pull out of me, and then I stood up, shoved him onto the chair, and climbed on top. "Again."

CHAPTER 17

ISABELLA

Three hours later, Roman had fallen asleep in Ryker's old bed at the Lycans' packhouse. I gazed at him from the doorway, yawning and desperately trying to keep my eyes open. We had fucked all night, and I had vowed not to succumb to sleep once tonight.

My heat hadn't shown up yet. I planned to keep it that way.

Completely exhausted from hours of going at it, my wolf lay quietly in the back of my mind, only whimpering every couple of minutes at me to go to sleep. But I couldn't allow myself to. I wanted to get through a night without heat and without Kylo.

He hadn't shown up once last night, and I thought that maybe Kylo had been telling the truth. His wolf was drawn to mine, not to me, not for desperation of being with someone, not to hurt Roman. Kylo's wolf wanted mine, and he couldn't stay away because of that. It wasn't him.

After shaking my head to rid my thoughts of him, I gently shut the door and walked to the large glass window that over-looked the entire training field. When I had first been here as a new recruit, I would look through these windows as the more advanced, better-trained Lycans completed eight hours of difficult training. At that time, I had been amazed at how the older Lycans could train for that long. But now, all of us trained hard for that long because we were fighting against a god who we knew nothing about and who was defeating us one wolf at a time, his corruption taking over our lands. All those people we had transported yesterday were alive, but their minds were gone and trapped.

Just like the Moon Goddess was probably right now.

Gaze flickering over the forest, I swallowed when I met the eyes of Kylo's wolf. He wasn't aggressively running at me and trying to mark me, like he usually was. He was just calmly waiting about fifty yards from the packhouse. How he had gotten onto the property without anyone noticing … I had no idea. But he was calm and had a manila folder in his mouth, canines lodged into it, as if he'd brought it for me.

I tied my robe tighter around my waist and walked down the stairs to the front door. Stepping out into the crisp morning air, I allowed myself to inhale his sweet scent and followed it through the woods to his wolf.

When I made it within ten feet of him, I stopped and nodded to him. "Shift."

Almost instantaneously, he transformed into his human and stood naked before me, taking the file from his mouth, biceps flexing. "You didn't go through your heat last night," Kylo said to me, a bit of what seemed like annoyance in his voice, though there wasn't any anger on his face.

"No," I whispered, wrapping my arms around myself.

"You were with Roman," he said.

Not knowing how he was going to react, I nodded slowly.

He clenched his jaw, growling almost instinctively under his breath, and then the calmness and the anger both seemed to dissipate quickly. "Were you having sex?"

My wolf slowly awoke inside of me, purring at the sight of a naked Kylo. Before I could stop her, she made me say, "Yes. Roman wants pups."

Pressing my lips together almost immediately, I scolded her inside my mind and gave him a tight smile. I didn't want to get him angry and possessive, like he had been the past few weeks.

"Pups?" Kylo snapped, taut chest flexing. "Do you want them?"

"Maybe …"

"Don't you think it's weird that he's trying to have pups with you during a *war*, Isabella?" Kylo asked me, one brow raised, yet he still didn't make a move toward me. The other night, he'd kept advancing, but now, he was stuck dead to the spot. "We're in the biggest war of our entire lives, and Roman wants to knock you up, so you're weak, so you're stuck with him."

I swallowed hard and narrowed my eyes. "I want pups too, Kylo."

"A couple weeks ago, you said that you'd told him you wanted to wait until after Dolus was defeated. Why are you letting him change your mind? Why are you letting him convince you to have pups—who'll be in danger—while Dolus is still thriving?"

"Kylo," I warned.

"If Dolus finds out you're pregnant with Roman's pup, he'll kill your child—that's assuming that Roman isn't Dolus himself. Otherwise, you'll be having a pup with a god who has been killing wolves left and fucking right."

"Can you stop trying to rip Roman and me apart?" I snapped, nails lengthening into claws and canines growing in my mouth, an undeniable rage pumping through me. Nothing could ever be fucking easy.

"Isabella, I'm trying to help you. You're too blinded to see what he's doing to you."

Unable to hold myself back, I slammed my hands into his chest to push him back and growled so loud that I wouldn't be surprised if Roman woke up and ran out here. "If you don't stop trying to break us up, I'm going to reject you," I said.

Almost immediately, he tensed. "Reject?"

The words had tumbled out of my mouth before I could stop them, but I didn't regret them at all. I'd meant everything that I said to him because I wasn't leaving Roman. He had been with me since we were children.

If Roman were really Dolus, I wouldn't care.

Well, I would because he had been hurting all these people. But Roman was mine and he'd never do anything like that. It wasn't in his nature to do something so sinister to anyone. He had seen what happened to his mother and wouldn't dare put that on someone else.

Either way, I didn't think I could reject Roman if he ended up being Dolus. That man had been mine for all this lifetime. And I didn't know if that was a good or bad thing anymore. My world felt too clouded, and with people speaking into my ears from all directions, it was hard to think for myself anymore.

"You'd reject me?" Kylo whispered, the anger on his face replaced with one of pity, sorrow, and terror. He tore his gaze away from me and stepped back, putting distance between us.

It looked like he actually believed Roman was corrupted.

"I'm trying to help you," he whispered, "because I love you."

Torn and frustrated with myself and with him, I rubbed a hand over my face. "I didn't mean to make you upset. I'm tired of you and Roman fighting with each other. You said it yourself—we're in the middle of a war. We need to think straight. This drama isn't helping."

"This drama is to keep you safe," Kylo said. "I don't want to see you dead or hurt because of this corruption, especially not by the hands of your mate. He's been more aggressive, Isabella—I know you see it. He could never defeat me in battle before, yet the other night, he grabbed me by the fucking neck and stopped me in his human form. He's asking for pups, has heightened sexual attraction. You still don't see it?"

I swallowed hard, my stomach tightening. "Can you please

leave?" I whispered, knowing that it was wrong but wanting a couple moments to think everything through. I needed sleep and a clear mind.

Sighing through his nose and refusing to look at me, he handed me the manila folder.

"What's this?" I asked.

"Information on Scarlett and some details I've gathered about how Roman got her back to his pack without a problem a couple weeks ago, all from witnesses in the area. Some of my pack members asked around. This is what I found."

My heart raced. "Is it bad?"

Kylo turned his back to me and started walking through the forest and back toward his property. "Why do you care? Roman can do no wrong in your eyes."

CHAPTER 18

KYLO

*a*nger rushed through my veins, fury through my limbs, pain through my heart. Everything I did was for her, and she continued to choose Roman over and over again without even looking at this whole situation from a logical point of view.

He wanted her to have his fucking pups—*his pups!*—in the middle of a fucking war.

If that didn't scream corrupt to her, I didn't know if anything could.

Stepping onto my property, I shifted into my human form, found some clothes in a house at the border, and stormed to the prison. I had a bone to pick with my prisoner because this didn't make fucking sense. Nothing did.

Isabella should've felt the heat last night. My wolf had.

He'd felt every agonizing second without his mate by his side.

After convincing the guards to take a break, I snatched the keys and locked the door behind me, so nobody could follow me in. Taking the same path I had last time, I kicked a rug out of the way, opened the hatch, and jumped down into the lower cellar. I lit a torch, the flame illuminating the dark crevices of the underground prison.

With light licking the cave walls, I followed the path toward the most secure cell in all of these woods. I had tried and tested it many, many times before to know that it was secure enough to hold someone with power like an alpha or something worse, like this woman.

When I reached my prisoner's cell, I set the torch down and kicked the metal bars. "Why didn't Isabella get her heat last night? I felt mine, but I couldn't feel her wolf. What happened to it? We are mates."

The woman stared up at me with a busted lip and an angry scowl. "You deserve it."

Unable to hold myself back, I grabbed her by the collar of her dress and pulled her into the air. "What the fuck happened? She's my mate, not his. Why didn't she feel the heat last night? Why can't she feel me?"

I screamed the words at her, but honestly, I was desperate. I wanted Isabella so fucking bad. Every night, my wolf went through heat too, called out for her wolf, aching to be by her side and spend eternity with her. I couldn't handle it anymore. She would never choose me, not in this lifetime and maybe not the next ones either.

Eternity alone was fucking ... lonely.

Always hoping that she'd change her mind, choose me.

My heart broke into even more pieces every moment that she wasn't mine again.

"Tell me how to fix it."

She laughed at me—fucking laughed—and then spit in my face. "You'll never fix it, you prick. Not until you let me out."

"On one condition."

"What?"

"Talk to Isabella for me."

She gritted her teeth. When I knew that she would agree, I released her, balled my hands into fists, and hurried out of the lower prison chambers with her following. Once I climbed the ladder to the upper cells, I closed the chamber door and pulled a dirty rug over it. She would talk to Isabella for me, then I would bring her right back here.

I didn't trust her, just like she shouldn't trust me.

CHAPTER 19

ISABELLA

"*W*ere you with Kylo?" Roman asked when I returned to the Lycans' packhouse.

My heart leaped, and I found myself scrambling to snap the file closed and holding it close to my chest. I hadn't gotten a chance to look through it yet. To be honest, I'd had a chance, but I didn't want to find anything incriminating on Roman. If I opened this folder up and found out that he had slept with Scarlett, I'd fucking lose it.

I could deal with almost anything else, but if he'd cheated on me …

"Yes," I said, placing the folder on the kitchen table and sitting on a chair. There wasn't any point in lying to him; Kylo's scent was all over my body, no matter how far away I'd tried to stay from him but couldn't. There was no washing it off in the river on my way back or taking a quick shower to hide it, and I didn't want to hide it either.

Roman tensed. "What did he want?"

"What he always wants."

"To mark you?"

After gnawing on the inside of my cheek, I quickly glanced down at the file. "Yes."

I wanted so badly to open it up and to prove to myself that Roman was a good guy. I trusted him so fucking much and knew he wouldn't do anything to hurt me, but there was always that voice in the back of my head, telling me otherwise. And that voice was my wolf's mate—Kylo. I couldn't shake the feeling that something was terribly off.

But I didn't know what that something was.

"And the file?" Roman asked, leaning against the kitchen counter.

"It's just … information on Dolus's whereabouts. Kylo thought he had something, but he doesn't. I've already gone over it numerous times." I glanced down at the file and shook my head. "Nothing."

Lie. Why did I lie to Roman?

Roman eyed me for a couple moments, and then he nodded and kissed me on the forehead. "I love you. I have to get back to the packhouse. We have training early this morning. Are you going to be okay here, all by yourself?"

I frowned, not wanting him to leave. My wolf had gotten her daily dose of Kylo, hopefully satisfied until tonight, and I so desperately wanted to sleep with Roman, have him hold me still while Dolus ruled my nightmares.

Instead of asking him to stay, I smiled weakly. "Yeah, I'll be fine."

Once he pressed another kiss on my forehead, he walked out the front door. I sat at the kitchen table and stared down at the folder for minutes, holding my fingers steady so they wouldn't tremble, but … I was so nervous, so freaking unsure, and so tired. I should've just gone to bed, called it a night, and read both the file about Roman and Scarlett *and* the file that Raj had given me last night about the Moon Goddess and divine wolves when I woke up.

But I ran to my office, grabbed Raj's file, and placed it on top of Roman's in the kitchen. I flipped open the top one and glossed over the images and drawings within the file of the divine wolves and of the Moon Goddess, who had a faint scar running down the side of her neck, almost one similar to a mate's bite.

I smiled at it, needing some good in my life before I opened Roman's file.

And when I was finished, I flipped open the file on Roman and stared down at the contents.

My stomach twisted.

My heart dropped.

"No," I whispered, shaking my head from side to side. "Please, don't let it be true."

I hurt so bad that even my wolf whimpered inside of me, and she hadn't whimpered about Roman in so long. Part of me thought that my wolf had lost her connection with him, but deep down she always still loved Roman. I was beginning to think that after last night, after he'd told us that he wanted pups, he was growing on her again. But this … this would break us.

"It's not true," I whispered to myself, aching to believe it. "It's not true. It's not true. It's not true. Roman wouldn't cheat on me. Roman wouldn't sleep with her. Roman loves me. Roman has loved me for years. He wouldn't do something like that."

But he hadn't told me how he had gotten Scarlett to come down to our pack.

"Mate," my wolf whimpered.

Mate.

For the first time in so freaking long, she recognized Roman as our mate. And our mate wouldn't do something like that to us. I had known Roman my entire life, and he had always protected us and even stopped dating other people once he found out that we were mates. He wouldn't cheat on me.

I didn't believe it.

"Mate," my wolf whispered through my mind again. *"Why would he do this?"*

"He wouldn't," I reassured. *"Kylo's men found the wrong information."*

They had to have.

After closing the folder, I walked to the bedroom, where Roman's scent still lingered on the sheets, crawled into bed, and wrapped myself up in his scent. Without thinking of something good, I would surely fucking lose it.

"Why doesn't mate love us?"

"He does."

"Why would he do that to us?"

"Why would he do that to us?" I repeated back at her, hoping she'd see there was no reason that Roman would ever cheat.

Roman loved us more than he loved anyone else. He always had.

My wolf stayed quiet for more than a couple moments but then said, *"Because I ... I haven't loved him like I should have. He must've done this to get back at me because of Kylo. But ... I've never stopped loving him. Kylo is my mate too, and I ... I'm sorry I did this to us."*

Chest tightening, I stared up at the ceiling and bit my lip to suppress a whimper. *"He didn't cheat on us,"* I said to her even though I said it more for myself. *"He wouldn't do that, no matter how much you want Kylo. He would be hurting both me and you. He's not that type of person. Tell me you know that."*

Again, she paused. *"I know."*

When the words tumbled through my mind, I finally relaxed against the mattress and closed my eyes. Though I could still feel the anxiety within her, I knew that she believed it deep down too. Roman would never intentionally hurt us or cheat with Scarlett.

CHAPTER 20

ISABELLA

I woke up with a startle, my heart racing and my body unmovable. Desperately, I tried to pull my arms off the bed, pull my legs to my chest, turn my body over, yet all I could do was twist my head to the side to see a bright light coming from the corner of the room.

When I squinted and readjusted my vision, I gasped. The Moon Goddess stood in the corner with a grand smile and a soft face, everything about her demanding my attention. And I wouldn't look away if she gave me the chance.

"How are you here?" I whispered. "I thought Dolus trapped you."

After a moment, she walked closer and nodded. "I am trapped in his hold."

"And in my bedroom?"

"You're dreaming, darling."

"Of you?"

"Who else?" she said, giving me a breathtaking smile. "We need to talk. Sit up."

When she lifted her finger for me to sit up, I found myself finally able to move my upper body again and sat against the headboard. I rarely dreamed anymore, and if I did, it was usually a nightmare about Dolus or Derek. Never a dream of the Moon Goddess.

"What do you want to talk about?" I asked.

"About finding me."

"We're doing everything that we can do," I said, running a hand over my face.

"You've done a lot." She paused. "But not everything."

"What more can we do? I've been working at the Lycans' nonstop and stayed up for days, trying to figure this all out. Roman is helping out as much as he can. Kylo is too. Tell me what I can do differently to help find you quicker because so many people are being controlled by Dolus. I'm scared that we're going to lose."

She walked around the room, her light following her and illuminating all the moonflowers that I'd decorated Ryker's old room with. It made it seem less like him and more of my space now because that was what it was. She paused at the window and stared out into the daylight.

Daylight.

I mean, I was taking a nap during the day, but … the light was still off-putting.

"What is there?" I asked again.

She set her lips into a tight line. "I granted you another mate for a reason, Isabella. You're stronger with Kylo by your side, but you continue to reject the mate bond. If you don't let him mark you soon, it will get to the point where it's going to hurt you and your wolf's soul."

My stomach twisted, chest tightening. "But I—"

"Isabella, you asked me what you can do, and I'm telling you exactly what needs to be done. If you don't mate with him, this entire world will collapse. You'll be infected with corruption, and then who can we trust? The leader of the Lycans will be unreliable, just as Ryker was. Everything you've worked for will go down the drain. The werewolf species will die, and it will be your fault."

I paused for a long moment and stared at the comforter, Roman's scent still drifting through the air. As much as I wanted everything to be fine without my mating Kylo, it wasn't going to be. I had been putting my wants and my needs above everyone, and I couldn't anymore.

"What do we do once we're mated?" I asked. "How will that change anything?"

She turned back to me, walked close enough to sit on the edge of the bed, and brushed a strand of hair off my face. "Oh, Isabella, don't you remember how it felt when you and Roman finally mated? All those elated emotions, feeling like you were complete and walking on the clouds, like you were almost unstoppable."

I nodded.

"With Kylo, it will be even better. Since you and he are the divine wolves, you *will be* unstoppable. Nobody will be able to even touch you, and you'll defeat Dolus in the snap of a couple fingers. You can't even grasp the amount of power that you'll possess when he sinks his teeth into your neck."

She brushed her fingers across the bare side of my neck, where Kylo would mark me. I shivered, not in delight, but in fear. If she was telling the truth, I was terrified that the bond I had with Roman would shatter into a million pieces. I couldn't let that happen, no matter what.

"You're still hesitant."

"Yes," I whispered. "I don't want Roman to leave me. I love him."

"But you love the werewolf species too, don't you?"

I paused and stared down at my lap, guilt washing over me.

She grabbed my chin and forced me to look up at her, her touch soft. "Don't you?"

"Yes."

After a moment, she smiled and pushed some hair behind her

ear. I glanced down at her neck and tensed when I saw that it was bare. No scar, no mark, like I had seen in the drawing of the Moon Goddess from Raj's file. Hell, I didn't remember seeing them the first time I'd met her at that party.

She drew her brows together. "Is there something wrong?"

I pulled my gaze away from her neck and smiled. "No. I'm just … nervous."

Nervous that this wasn't the Moon Goddess at all.

The artist of the original drawings might've added that aspect to show just how important a mate's bite was, but the readings and ancient text had talked briefly about it too. This woman sitting in front of me wasn't the Moon Goddess, and this wasn't a dream.

This was real, and she was a fraud.

CHAPTER 21

ISABELLA

"*I* shall leave you now, Isabella," the Moon Goddess fraud said.

She stood and walked over to the bedroom door, her white dress blowing after her so beautifully that if it wasn't for her markless neck, I would've believed that the Moon Goddess had visited my dreams and that I really had to let Kylo mark me to protect the world.

After straightening my back, I said, "Wait," because I wanted her to stay here for as long as humanly possible.

Sooner or later, Raj would come into the packhouse to wake me for practice and work today. I wanted him to see her too.

"What is it, my dear?" she asked, glancing over her shoulder.

"Please, stay with me. Tell me what else I have to do."

"I cannot stay any longer. Dolus will figure out that I have visited you in your dreams. And if he plucks me out forcefully, he will know everything I told you, especially what I told you needs to be done."

The "Moon Goddess" talked so surely that I almost believed her.

Whoever this woman really was … she was damn good at

what she did.

"Please," I whispered, crawling to the edge of the bed. "Stay."

"I must go." She opened the bedroom door. "Good luck."

And with that, she was gone.

As soon as my bedroom door closed, I shut my eyes and forced the mind link to Raj, hoping that he was on the Lycans' territory.

His voice came through in a sigh, as if he was scolding someone for doing something wrong. *"Hello?"*

"Raj, you have to listen to me. There is a woman exiting the Lycans' packhouse now. She claimed to be the Moon Goddess but is a fraud. I need you to figure out where she is going. Follow her, but don't let her see you and don't leave a trail of your scent behind you. And most importantly, do not engage."

Just through the mind link, I could feel Raj tense. *"Is everything okay? Did she hurt you?"*

"No, but you have to go now before she disappears. We need information on her. I'll let you know what's going on later tonight. I have to go speak to Roman. Please, don't let me down. This is our first clue of possibly finding Dolus."

Once he grunted on the other end, I glanced out the window to see the woman disappearing north through the woods and pulled on some pants. This was freaking bad—so bad. I had been listening to that woman since the party. Who knew if what she'd said was a lie or if it was truth? Honestly, I couldn't believe any of it right now.

For all I knew, Kylo wasn't my divine mate. And I wasn't a divine wolf.

A sinking feeling spread throughout my body. But then why would my wolf react to Kylo the way that she did? She wouldn't be telling me that he was our mate if he wasn't. Maybe she was hypnotized or … or something because none of this made any damn sense.

When I decided that the coast was clear, I sprinted down the stairs, out of the house, and into the woods, hurrying toward my pack. Roman's scent lingered in the air still, and the thought of Kylo telling me that Roman had cheated made me feel like shit.

It wasn't true in the slightest—I knew that.

But I needed to know what had happened when he captured Scarlett. Had he had to do something to her? Had he seen something while he was out? Was what had happened so scarring that Roman didn't want to remember it in the slightest?

Fifteen minutes later, I ran up to the property to see the warrior wolves training. Roman stood among them with sweat dripping down his taut chest and the sunlight glistening off him, like it would with a god. I stood back and admired him for a mere moment, knowing that this man wouldn't do anything to hurt me.

Roman spotted me from across the field and paused, brows drawn together. "Isabella?"

Unable to stop myself, I ran over to him and pulled him into a tight hug, fear rushing through me at the thought of being alone with that woman in the Lycans' packhouse. If she could get inside without being spotted, who knew what else she was capable of?

"What's wrong?" he asked, taking my face in his hands. "What happened?"

"You need to tell me everything that happened when you captured Scarlett."

He paused. "Isabella, I—"

"Now!" I shouted and then immediately regretted it. "Sorry, but I need to know. Now."

Grasping my hand, he pulled me toward the packhouse. I stepped in and hurried to his office, shutting the door behind us both.

"We don't have time to waste anymore. Tell me what you don't want to. I promise that I won't hate you and that I'll believe you."

"You will hate me," Roman whispered, voice suddenly full of

vulnerability.

"Tell me," I pleaded, grabbing his hand and holding it to my heart. "I know whatever you did was to protect me. I could never hate you—ever. Please, trust me with this or … or …" I hated even *thinking* this. "Or my wolf will force me to believe what Kylo told me—that you cheated. And I know you would never do that to me."

Roman shook his head, tears filling his eyes. "I would never cheat on you, Isabella. When I was there, I saw and did shit that I don't want to remember. People were dead, and Scarlett wouldn't leave with me unless I proved myself to her, so I … she forced me to …"

We gave each other strength to get through the worst things in our lives, and I knew that this was one of them.

So, I stroked my fingers against his hair and kissed him softly. "What did you do?"

"She made me kill an innocent fucking boy." A tear slid down his cheek. "I'm sorry. I shouldn't have done it. I couldn't get her to trust me any other way. I'm a fucking terrible person, so fucking shitty. I should've told you sooner. I've tried to block it out for so long."

My heart broke, but it didn't change the way I felt about him. Next to nothing would.

Instead, I pulled him closer to me and rested his head on my shoulder, letting my alpha cry his eyes out and finally … finally come to terms with what he'd done. And as bad as it was, he'd had no choice but to do it to gain the upper hand. Or at least, that was before I'd found out that the Moon Goddess was a fraud.

"I don't hate you for that," I said to him. "But I need to tell you something. Someone … someone made it into the Lycans' pack-house and claimed to be the Moon Goddess. She had been at the party with Kylo too. I don't know what to believe anymore, but all I know is that she's a fraud and that I don't trust Kylo anymore. We need to figure this out—together."

CHAPTER 22

ISABELLA

"We have to figure this out," I said to Roman, grabbing his hand and leading him up the steps toward Kylo's packhouse.

From his intense, lingering scent on the sidewalk, he had to be here, and we couldn't wait much longer to hear from Raj. I needed to do my own investigating.

"This isn't the way to do it," Roman said, tightening his fingers around mine.

"Do you have another suggestion?" I stared up at Kylo's door, my stomach in knots. When Roman didn't answer me, I lifted my fist and knocked on the door. "I'm sorry, Roman, but this needs to be handled as quickly as possible. We don't have another way right now. When we do, we will—"

The door swung open, and Kylo stood in front of us with his hair disheveled.

I gave him a small smile and released Roman's hand, stepping closer to him. "Kylo," I said, letting my wolf purr slightly—very slightly so it wouldn't come off as suspicious. "Can we come in? I think we all have some things we need to talk about."

When he glanced from me to Roman, his gaze hardened. I

grabbed his hand in an attempt to convince him that this was for the best.

And thankfully, he looked back at me and smiled. "Anything for you."

Opening the door wider, he stepped back and let us walk into his home. It was weird, being here again, and I was … uncomfortable, to say the least. Honestly, I didn't know if being here was a bad idea or not. All I knew was that I hated freaking waiting.

Once we sat on the white leather couches in the living room, I cleared my throat. "I wanted to apologize. I didn't mean to snap at you earlier and tell you that I was going to reject you. My wolf is ready to be marked, but I need a bit more time." I leaned closer to him and grabbed his hand. "I hope you understand that it's not you."

Kylo let out a long sigh through his mouth. "It's my fault. I shouldn't have pushed it on you. I can't control myself any longer. I've waited so long for you, princess. I don't want to wait another moment, but I will, if that's what you need."

A moment passed in complete silence, neither Roman nor I knowing what to say next. We hadn't really come over here with much of a plan other than to gain Kylo's trust again and figure out what the hell was going on. But gaining his trust could mean so many things.

"Did you get a chance to look in that file I gave you?" Kylo asked.

Pretending that it hadn't affected me, I shook my head. "Not yet. I didn't get any sleep last night, so I took a nap today. And, uh, the Moon Goddess visited me in my dream actually. I wanted to come and tell you."

Sitting up taller, Kylo looked livelier at the mention of the Moon Goddess. "She did?"

I nodded. "At least, the ghost of her or something. She's really trapped in Dolus's hold. She told me … that we are the only ones who can defeat Dolus—*together*. We have to get her out, and … that means that you'll have to mark me soon."

Kylo tried hard to hide his grin, but he couldn't.

Moving closer to him, I tugged Roman along. "I thought that it would be best for all of us if we … took a day for ourselves to get to know each other a bit better. Maybe the more I learn about you"—I brushed a strand of his brown hair off his forehead—"the more comfortable I'll be with letting you mark me."

"I agree," Roman finally said. "We've been through fucking hell already. I've just been more stressed than usual. I wanted to apologize too. Let's have food and then we can"—Roman glanced at me, his eyes dark and his fingers snaking around my waist, as if to insinuate more—"see where things lead."

Kylo glanced from Roman to me, eyes softening. "All right then, let's see where today takes us."

CHAPTER 23

ROMAN

"*We need to distract Kylo for a while longer,*" Isabella said through the mind link. *"And to find out everything we can. He was trying to make you look guilty for a reason. Raj is doing some research for me. Please, just go along with it."*

I would listen to my mate because she knew more about this than I did, but that didn't mean I fucking liked any of this. In fact, I wanted to reach across the restaurant table and snap Kylo's neck into two fucking pieces.

Kylo smiled at Isabella—*my* Isabella—so innocently and like he hadn't tried to frame me for supposedly cheating on her. If he knew anything about me, he'd fucking know that I would never do such a goddamn thing. I loved Isabella more than he ever could. I had even let him touch her because that was what she wanted. I shouldn't have. I knew that now.

After this, nobody would ever touch her again. She was mine.

"*Roman, please,*" Isabella pleaded through the link.

"*Fine,*" I growled, putting on my best smile and placing a hand on her thigh.

Isabella tensed briefly, glancing over at me and asking me

what I was doing with those beautiful eyes of hers. My lip curled into a smile, and I breathed in her scent to calm myself as I moved even closer to her.

"Remember what happened last time we were here?" I asked, looking over at Kylo and holding my anger back.

Isabella shot me a sideways glare. *"What are you doing?"*

"Pretending for you."

My hand slid up her thigh and dipped underneath the skirt she had worn for Kylo today. As much as I fucking hated it, I knew that letting him see her again might be the only way he would give us any information. But I'd do anything in my power to hold off on that right now.

So, I brushed two fingers against her panties and smirked at Kylo, who still looked a bit hesitant or as if he was analyzing, not believing that I really wanted this to happen. I had to make it fucking believable if this was going to work. Hopefully, Raj would have something soon.

"You remember the way Isabella's cunt smelled last time?" I asked him. "Better than any lunch could." I slipped a couple fingers into her panties and rubbed her clit until her pussy was sopping on my fingers. I wrapped my free hand around her throat and looked down at her. "You were a mess that afternoon. Couldn't even speak coherently to our waiter." I glanced up to see a woman with an apron walking this way. "Let's see how you do this time."

"Roman," Isabella squealed, grasping my hand. "Please, let's just—"

When the waitress walked over with a big smile on her face, I pulled my hand away from Isabella's throat, keeping the other stuffed between her pussy lips, and gave the woman my best smile. "How are you?"

"Good, Alpha. You?"

"Oh, I'm wonderful."

It was both a lie and the truth. If I could be anywhere else now that wasn't across from Kylo, I'd be there in a heartbeat, but the way Isabella's pussy just fucking salivated on me was sexy as fuck. She always came the hardest when someone watched even if it was this asshole.

"What would you all like today? We have a couple of specials."

"Ladies first," Kylo said, keeping an intent stare on Isabella, his eyes barely peeling away from her for a mere moment. "What would you like, Isabella?"

Isabella dug her fingers into my wrist harder, but I didn't stop just because she inflicted a little pain on me. Her claws in my wrist made me want to make her scream, cry out, beg for me and only me. Right here. Right in front of Kylo, this waitress, and everyone else.

"I, um, I …" Isabella sucked in a sharp breath, pale cheeks flushing. "I—"

Her entire body tensed, and she pressed her thighs together.

"We're waiting," I said.

"I haven't even looked at the m-m-menu." She stared down at the menu that she had looked at for a solid twenty minutes when we got here. She hadn't known what to say to Kylo earlier, and gaping at the menu was the only thing she *could* do.

My fingers slipped into her tight cunt and curled at just the right angle, hitting her G-spot.

"I'll do the steak," she said quickly, whimpering toward the end.

The waitress scribbled something on her notepad and looked back up. "How would you like that done?"

"Medium."

"And mashed potatoes and green beans or—"

"Goddamnit," Isabella said through the mind link, her pussy clenching on my three large fingers massaging her G-spot. *"You're going to make me fucking come."*

"Whatever is fine!" Isabella grabbed her water and took a huge gulp, biting down on the straw and whimpering again.

After Kylo and I ordered our food, I pulled the water away from Isabella and forced her to sit back in the booth, showing her flushed body to Kylo because he wasn't breaking as easily as he had last time. It was either he didn't like me touching her or he didn't believe that we would actually be on speaking terms again.

And I hoped to the Goddess that he wasn't onto us.

"Tell me what you see, Kylo," I commanded, needing him to break at least for a little while. I didn't want to do this for the rest of the night, the rest of the week, and certainly not for the rest of my life. "What's Isabella look like to you?"

Kylo sat back and crossed his arms over his chest, eyes flickering down Isabella's body. And then he finally curled his lips into that smirk he'd always had with Scarlett when they were a thing. I knew we were close to breaking him for a moment, to him letting his guard down.

"Like a sopping, drooling little mess."

With wide eyes, Isabella wiped the drool off her lip and blushed. "Oh, Goddess."

"She's hungry for cock, isn't she?" I asked.

Kylo sucked in a sharp breath and pushed a hand underneath the table, probably to relieve himself. I grabbed Isabella's hand and placed it on the bulge in my pants, making her rub me off until she whimpered.

"Oh, please," she whispered, looking up at me. "Please, let me come. I need to come."

I grabbed her chin and forced her to look at Kylo. "You ask him."

Kylo grunted underneath his breath. There it was.

"Please, Kylo," Isabella murmured. "Can I come? Please?"

Kylo stared at her for a few moments, eyes flashing gold, and his wolf finally came out, which meant that we had done something to break him, to get him to trust us slightly again. He grunted in response, giving a slight nod of his head, and she slapped a hand over her mouth, letting out a throaty moan as her legs convulsed around me.

This wasn't much, but it was something.

CHAPTER 24

ISABELLA

"*L*unch was lovely," I said to the waitress as she took our plates. "Thank you."

All throughout lunch, Roman had kept playing with me because he thought it would break Kylo to pieces for me, and honestly, it was a start. He had become more friendly compared to when we had shown up at his packhouse this morning, both in nerves.

I just hoped that he wasn't onto us.

"So …" I leaned forward, wondering what the fuck to say.

Roman was better at this than I was, but maybe that was because he knew Kylo more than I did. He knew what would break him. He seemed to know more than even my wolf, who had been oddly quiet all morning.

"What are you doing today, Kylo? Any plans, or did you clear them all out for us?"

Kylo placed his napkin on the table and sat back against the booth, his muscles flexing under his polo shirt. I let my gaze linger for a moment more than I should've, knowing that Kylo loved when I stared at him. Any sort of affection from me, he loved.

"I have a couple prisoners that I need to check up on, but other than that …" Kylo started, giving me a smile and tilted forward to capture my hand.

Roman tensed next to me, but I grabbed his hand under the table with my free one to calm him down. This needed to work. We had spent all morning with him and made such little progress, but it was something. No turning back now. So, I let Kylo intertwine our fingers.

"You're all I have on the schedule."

"Me and Roman?"

Kylo drew in a heavy breath and looked over at Roman, who pulled his hand away from mine and wrapped it around my waist.

Kylo paused for a long moment and then finally nodded. "You and Roman, but that's it. Nobody else in this mix. Not today."

After looking down at his watch, Kylo cleared his throat. "I should check up on them now. I'll meet you back at the pack-house in twenty minutes."

My mind link suddenly buzzed, Raj's voice coming through for the first time in hours. For a while, I thought that the woman who had visited me this morning found out about him and killed him. That wouldn't be good at fucking all.

"Isabella, I followed that woman," he started. *"She disappeared into what looked like an underground prison. I slipped into the passageway that she'd walked into and couldn't find her down there at all. I lost all scent of her. It was like she disappeared completely."*

An underground prison? In the middle of a forest?

I looked up at Kylo, stomach turning, and smiled at him. "Can we come with you?"

Raj spoke some more. *"The prison was empty. Looked like it had been for hundreds of years, but I smelled tons of silver somewhere, though the prison wasn't made of* that *many silver cells, so I don't know where it was coming from."*

"Where was it? At Kylo's?"

"No," Raj said. *"Near Scarlett's old packhouse."*

After listening to his words, I leaned forward to urge Kylo to let us come with him. Kylo had an underground prison that seemed like the same setup. I had been down there once or twice within the past couple weeks and caught scent of heaps of silver. The cells were made of silver, but by the intense smell, there had to be more. I knew it to be true.

Even if Kylo wasn't hiding anything and was completely innocent, maybe I could analyze his prison because it seemed similar. Maybe I could figure out where that woman had gone because she was no god. She shouldn't be able to poof out of a room in the snap of a couple fingers.

"Sure," Kylo said after a moment.

So, we all slid out of the booth and followed Kylo toward the prison. Every step we took, my stomach tightened more and more. Something didn't feel completely right because I'd expected Kylo to refuse, to hide information. But he was so open for me to see everything that he had.

My expectations about what he'd do and his actions didn't match.

And it made me uneasy.

After the guards opened the double doors for us, we wandered down into the prison. Kylo flicked the light on, and prisoners grunted and roared in response to the brightness. He pushed some cobwebs out of the way and grabbed my hand to lead me down the creaky stairs.

Every cell, every room that we went in or passed by, I looked into, inspecting as much as I could without looking suspicious about it. I didn't want Kylo to know anything just yet, not even that I'd figured out the Moon Goddess woman wasn't the real Moon Goddess.

"Distract Kylo for a second," I said to Roman through the mind link.

He furrowed his brows down at me and then took a couple

steps forward to match Kylo's strides, falling into a conversation with him. I expected them to both blow up at each other, but for once, they were actually talking about war and wolves and prisoners. Not me.

While they walked ahead, I stayed behind and looked around, smelling the thick scent of silver in one specific area. I walked into the room and scanned it, wondering where the hell it was coming from.

I pushed some shelves to the side, looked under furniture, on top of messy tables.

Nothing.

And when I heard Roman and Kylo returning, I cursed under my breath and pulled up a rug as my last damn hope to find *anything* that could give me answers to where that woman had gone. I didn't know where the hell the woman had really gone, or if Kylo took them to the same place, but… the layouts of the prisons were identical.

My eyes widened at the hatch underneath the rug.

A hatch that could lead *anywhere*.

A hatch that smelled like silver.

CHAPTER 25

ISABELLA

*A*lphas sat in the Lycans' auditorium, talking loudly, their voices filled with worry. The Lycans tried to calm them down as much as they could, but the ones who were violent, pushing and shoving, we labeled them as corrupted and detained them. I wasn't taking any chances. If they couldn't act civil, then they'd be treated as wild animals.

I glanced at Kylo and Roman sitting in the first row and tightened my fist behind the podium.

It had been three days—three fucking days—since I'd found that hatchet in Kylo's prison. And still, no matter the amount of time that had passed, no matter what kind of plan I'd thought up, I hadn't been able to get back down into his prison without him coming with me or without him getting suspicious.

And as strong as I was—I had trained for years to become a Lycan and taken down the bad guys—I wasn't stupid. If Kylo was *Dolus*—I hoped that he wasn't, but I had a sinking feeling in my stomach that Kylo had known about the fake goddess all along and was therefore hiding *a lot* more from me—I hadn't anything about him or his powers at the time.

Who knew what Dolus was capable of?

But after a few of days of locking myself in the Lycans' pack-house and studying every book and every scholar's work on Dolus and the divine wolves, I had come to know him and his powers a bit better.

Let me tell you … he was terrifying. Master of deception and treachery, trickery and craftiness, Dolus had lied through his very teeth and deceived the world better than anyone else could. And it wasn't just humans he'd tricked, but gods too. *Gods.* Roman and I were just mortals.

If he wanted to destroy us, he could in a moment's notice.

That was if Kylo was Dolus.

Which was one of the reasons I'd called an alpha meeting today to talk about Dolus and how we would defeat him for good this time. I needed other people around for when Roman and I launched the secret plan we had thought up last night. It didn't get us any closer to opening that hatch, but maybe … it would start to show Kylo's true colors—if he was Dolus.

As the meeting came to a midday break, I cleared my throat. "Naomi."

I motioned for her to come forward, keeping my gaze on Roman, who looked uneasy or nervous next to Kylo. He hadn't torn his gaze away from me once today and was enacting this plan perfectly so far.

Naomi hopped up from her seat and hurried over to the front. Behind the podium, I handed her a note, which she unraveled and stared up at me with big eyes. If she was a wolf, this could've been more discreet—a couple words through the mind link—but we couldn't do that now. Maybe she'd become a wolf one day.

She showed me the note, eyebrows raised. "You really want me to do this alone?"

After taking back the note that read, *Watch Beta Roger from Kylo's pack*, I ripped it into small pieces that nobody would ever read. Sprinkled some on the auditorium floor behind the podium and placed the rest in my pocket, so even if someone tried reading it, they wouldn't get the full message.

"No, you'll complete this mission with Oliver." I glanced at Oliver, who sat in the back of the room, nodding toward Naomi.

Naomi blushed and looked back at me, nodding in approval.

Before she could run off, I grasped her hand. "Don't let me down. This is the most important mission that you will ever go on."

"I promise I won't let you down."

And because I knew that Kylo was listening to every word of our conversation, I said, "Now, go. We don't have much time. I need you to find all the information that you can about Scarlett's old pack. We have a lead."

Once Naomi ran off in Oliver's direction, I told the alphas that we had to take a break for five minutes and that there were refreshments in our front room. Last time, they had bled us dry of alcohol and food, but … it was either that or we didn't figure any of this out.

So, I hopped off the stage and walked toward Roman and Kylo, my stomach in tight knots at the thought of actually enacting this plan with Roman. It was beyond crazy. Kylo could snap. Dolus could emerge from the shadows. But it needed to be done.

Almost immediately, Roman stood from his seat and protectively wrapped his arm around my waist, digging his fingers into my side a bit too tightly.

Kylo glanced down at them, jaw twitching briefly, and then stood. "A lot of alphas have been corrupted."

"Too many," I said, glancing behind him and stepping away from Roman. "I should go check on them. Raj will need my help, and I—"

"No," Roman growled, possessiveness dripping from his voice.

Again, Kylo noticed and stared at him for longer than usual.

I shifted uncomfortably beside Roman and tore his fingers off me. "Roman, it's fine. I'm just going to be a few minutes."

"I don't want you to be corrupted."

"I won't."

"Isabella," Roman scolded softly. "Let Raj take care of it. I know you want to save the day, but you have to rest. You've been up for the past three days, trying to find Dolus. If you don't sleep, he might take you away from me. And I can't lose someone else I care about. I'm not going to allow it."

"I thought we were over this, Roman," I snapped.

"You thought we were, but I'm not over it. I'll never be over it. You keep putting yourself in harm's way."

Oh, Roman was good at playing make-believe.

After letting out a sigh through my nose, I shook my head. "We've talked about this so many times, Roman. I have to tie up some loose ends with these alphas, and I'll be back. It'll be five minutes, max."

Roman's lips twitched, and he growled again. "You never listen."

"And you don't trust me." I looked over at Kylo. "Watch him for a couple moments. Calm him down. I have work to take care of." And with that, I hurried out of the auditorium before I made it obvious that this was all an act, that our little fight had been planned, that Roman's over-the-top display of possessiveness wasn't what Kylo thought it was.

CHAPTER 26

"*Y*ou sure this is going to work?" Raj asked through the mind link.

From the Lycans' packhouse front yard, I watched Naomi and Oliver disappear through the forest and head to Kylo's packhouse. I hoped to the Goddess that everything was going to work, that our plan was foolproof, but who the hell knew what was going to happen to us?

I sure as hell didn't.

"No," I said honestly.

I hopped onto the porch stairs to get back to the meeting before Kylo and Roman blew up into a huge argument. By the way Kylo had glared at Roman earlier when he was touching me, I knew Kylo was going to say something to him or to me about Roman not trusting me still, and I needed to stay calm.

"How many are corrupted as of today?" I asked Raj.

"Too many," Raj said, rubbing his hand across his face. "Almost fifty percent of wolves who live in our forest. Thankfully, Jane and Vanessa are slowly coming back to normal, but … Derek is still gone somewhere. One of our wolves caught a scent of him last night while you were studying the file on Dolus."

My eyes widened. "Derek?"

"Yes, Derek—and not the ghost of him either. The real Derek."

"Do you think he's …" I paused and listened for any lurkers in the forest, and then I continued through the mind link, just in case. Nobody could find out the information that Raj and I knew. We hadn't even told any of the other Lycans yet. *Do you think he's in one of those underground hatches? Locked in a silver cage?*

Raj blew a breath out of his nose and walked with me back into the auditorium. *I hope so. Either way, we need to gather a team and head back to the cage in Scarlett's packhouse. I don't want anyone to go down there alone. We don't know what kind of fucked up shit is in those underground prisons.*

"The Moon Goddess maybe."

He smiled just a bit. *Maybe.*

Suddenly, he stiffened. *Someone is watching.*

Instead of gazing over my shoulder like I wanted to, I cleared my throat. "Send warriors to check it out throughout the day. This could be a lead." Lie. "Let me know what's going on, and we can go from there."

After nodding and whispering, "Good luck," to me, Raj departed from the auditorium.

I turned around to see Kylo standing mere feet from me now, his big brown eyes fixed on me. And for a moment, I had to hush my wolf when she purred at the sight of him.

"Find anything?"

"A possible lead."

I placed my hand on his chest and reminded myself that I needed to find a way into that hatch. And as a Lycan, I knew I had to do whatever that was to uncover what was really going on. And anything meant *anything.*

"You're not going out with them?" Kylo asked with his arms crossed over his chest and a small smile on his face. "Is the leader of the Lycans afraid of what she'll find out there?"

My breath caught in my throat—and not in a good way. I

couldn't understand if Kylo was poking fun at me or if he was sincerely asking if I was afraid of Dolus. Hell, because he had a prison inside of a prison filled with silver, he could mean anything.

"Remember the plan," Roman said through our mind link, glancing at us from down the aisle. Even with my back turned, I knew that he was watching, could feel his gaze burning into me. He didn't like me being alone with Kylo. *"Don't get angry."*

"No, I'm not afraid, but Roman isn't going to let me out of his sight," I said.

I placed my hand on my stomach, shook my head, and stopped in the center of the room. After glancing over my shoulder at Roman, I gnawed on the inside of my lip.

If anything happened and Kylo exploded into the terrifying Dolus, we were surrounded by tons of uncorrupted alphas and the strongest warriors to defend our lands. I had to believe that we'd all do anything in our power to stop him. Dolus had our Goddess trapped.

Kylo cleared his throat. "I hate to tell you this again, but Roman doesn't believe in you and your abilities. He thinks you're weak, Isabella. Why can't you see that? He will never be half the fucking man that I could be for you. And I gave you proof. You read that file I gave you, right?"

"Yes," I whispered, thinking back to the lies Kylo had tried to feed me. "I read it last night, but it's not that simple."

"It is simple. He cheated on you. He's using you. What can possibly—"

Before he could finish his sentence, I placed my hands on his chest to shut him up. "I'm pregnant with Roman's pup."

CHAPTER 27

KYLO

"No." I balled my hands into fists and shook my head, rage bursting through the calm facade I had put on for the past few weeks.

This couldn't be happening. Isabella couldn't be pregnant, especially not with Roman's fucking pup.

"Please, don't make a scene," Isabella whispered.

But all I wanted to do was rip this packhouse apart. I wanted to tear everyone inside into two pieces and finally claim Isabella for myself because I had waited so long for her. And I was so fucking close to having her as mine again.

"How can I not make a scene?" I growled. "Roman cheated on you, never believes in your abilities, and will always stop you from succeeding and becoming the woman you were meant to be. And now, you're pregnant with his pup!"

"Kylo," Isabella said, grasping my bicep and digging her claws into me to ground me.

After all this time, she knew exactly how to make me calm, no matter how much I wanted to rip someone's throat out and kill them.

She inched closer to me and lowered her voice. "Please, stay calm. I need your help."

"My help?" I asked, desperately keeping my anger suppressed right now.

And while I wanted to be angry with Roman, I was more furious with myself. I had waited too fucking long to be with her. She'd grow apart from me and now raise pups with Roman and Roman only.

Isabella pulled me farther away from Roman and out on to the patio by ourselves. "After Roman found out this morning, he's become so much more possessive, especially when I'm around other people. I'm afraid that he might … that he might …"

My heart ached for my mate. "That he might what?"

"That he might hurt me," she whispered with tears in her eyes. "On accident."

She hugged her arms around her body and walked farther onto the patio and away from the door, shaking her head and staring at her feet. "You saw how he was in there with you. What if he picks a fight with someone, loses control, and accidentally hurts me or the baby?"

Hands balled into fists, I glared through the window at Roman, wanting nothing more than to end his life. I should've done it long before today. He fucking deserved it for what he had done to Scarlett and what he had taken from me before.

"I'll keep you safe, Isabella," I said through gritted teeth. "And I'll take care of him too."

This could be my chance to show Isabella that Roman meant nothing to her, that I was the only person she would ever need in any lifetime. This wasn't about fated mates anymore; it was about who loved her more. And, fucking Goddess, I did.

She placed her hands on top of my fists. "Please, I don't want you to hurt him. Let me handle Roman. I just … I need you to keep me safe."

"I won't hurt Roman," I lied.

Piercing blue eyes and an arched brow said she didn't believe me.

Isabella shook her head. "Kylo, you have to promise me that you won't hurt him at all. If you hurt him, you'll be hurting me, and ... and I know that you love me, and I love you too ..."

Fuck.

Those words.

Those fucking words.

I had been waiting to hear them again since forever.

Gods, those words made everything better. They always had.

She continued talking, but I didn't hear a word that she said. Instead of listening, I brushed a strand of her hair out of her face with my pinkie finger and felt my heart warm. Isabella always felt so right. It didn't matter what we did, who we were, she was always it.

After placing her hand over mine, she smiled. "No matter what happens, you have to let me deal with Roman. I will sort him out. I just need you to protect me for a bit. Promise me, Kylo. You have to promise."

"I promise," I whispered, placing my hands on her hips and tugging her closer, like I should've been doing from the first day I laid eyes on her. "I'd do anything for you, princess. *Anything.*"

Once she glanced over her shoulder at Roman in the pack-house, she gnawed on the inside of her lip. "Roman won't let me out of his sight, but ... I might be able to get away from him for the night if I tell him I have duties with the Lycans. But ... I'm not sure."

"Tell Roman that this is the only way to find the Moon Goddess, that you have a commitment to me, your divine mate too. You need to do this for the species of the werewolf race, not for him. We're all depending on you."

Hesitantly, she nodded. I could just feel the nerves bubbling up under her skin. "Okay ..."

"And then come meet me at my packhouse. You can stay in my home for however long you'd like."

Isabella grinned at me and threw her arms around my shoulders, pulling me into a hug. "Thank you, Kylo. I owe you so much," she whispered into my ear. "And I'll be sure to repay you by the time this is all over. You won't have to wait much longer for me."

And for a moment, I thought that Isabella had mastered the ways of Dolus himself and become a pro at deception and lying right through her pearly white canines, but then my mind changed when I smelled it.

Two scents.

Both coming from Isabella's belly.

CHAPTER 28

ROMAN

"*I*'m not letting you go."

Isabella placed a hand on my chest, just as we had rehearsed. "Roman, please."

We stood in front of Kylo, my hand tightly holding her wrist and my heart pounding in my chest. If we were going to make this performance believable enough for Kylo, then I had to act like the possessive asshole that I was.

"You don't need to go. You work yourself into the ground. Let someone else handle this."

"No!" Isabella shouted, pulling herself away from me. "I will not let my Lycans do the work themselves. When I took over this pack, I dedicated my time to them. I love you, but I'm trying to save our species and the world."

I took a domineering step toward her, growling underneath my breath. Kylo stepped between us and placed his hand on my chest, shoving me away.

"Don't touch her again," Kylo said, canines emerging from underneath his lips. "She can make her own decisions."

Instead of letting him talk me down—because I would never let him, even when I wasn't acting—I shoved him back and into

Isabella, cursing myself when she squealed. She grasped on to his bicep, breath catching, and stumbled back.

Kylo shoved me harder against the side of the house, taking my shirt collar in his hands and holding me tightly. "Fucking control yourself before I do something about it, Roman. Your chances are running the fuck out with me."

After pushing Kylo away from me, I readjusted my shirt and looked at Isabella. "You'd better come back to the packhouse right when you finish, or I'll have our entire pack out looking for you. Do you understand?"

Isabella, who was usually headstrong, placed a hand over her stomach. "I'll come back, Roman. Now, please, go and let me do business."

I threw one last dirty look toward Kylo and walked back into the Lycans' packhouse with Raj, my hands balled into tight fists and my wolf aching to take control and kill that animal right here and right now. I didn't know if I'd be able to wait any longer.

It was all supposed to be one big fat lie, a put-on, an act to distract Kylo, but when we had woken up today, Isabella had smelled different. It wasn't just her usually woodsy scent, but also a hint of something—or someone—else. And I didn't like the thought of Isabella being with Kylo the entire night if she really was pregnant.

"Isabella probably hasn't told you, but we found some clues as to where Derek could be," Raj said, handing me a file and glancing over my shoulder at Kylo and Isabella outside. He stared at them for a couple moments and tensed, giving me a quick look that said he didn't trust him either. "We're leaving in fifteen minutes. Look over the folder and then gather your warriors."

Before he had a chance to leave, I grabbed his shoulder and pulled him back. "Do you think she's safe with him? Tell me what you really think about Kylo and how he fits into all of this. I need to know that we're not the only ones who think he's a bit off."

Raj grimaced and blew out a breath. "Everything with him was a bit too convenient."

Convenient.

That was what I'd call it too.

Just as Dolus had needed to be found and corruption started, Kylo had shown back up in my life with a need to take my mate away. And … the Moon Goddess … how could she have even paired them up? Who knew if she had or if Dolus had forced her to?

I didn't trust Kylo at all.

Outside the house, Kylo placed his hand on Isabella's lower back and guided her down the stairs. I stared through the window at them with my teeth clenched.

"I'm going to kill him one of these days," I growled under my breath.

"Not if Isabella kills him first."

Raj laughed, but I didn't find anything funny about this. Kylo still had the fucking flower that could kill her in a moment's notice. And if he did have powers beyond measure, then he might already be on to us.

"Don't worry about Isabella," Raj said to me, nodding toward the forest. "We need to go find Derek. He's out in these woods somewhere, and I'm not going into those underground prison chambers by myself."

After taking one last lingering look in the direction Isabella had disappeared, I howled to myself and followed Raj and a couple other Lycans toward Scarlett's old packhouse, where they had discovered an underground prison a couple days ago. We would find Derek, and Isabella would figure out what the fuck was up with Kylo.

I trusted her to do so.

But it wasn't only Isabella that worried me. Something dark and feral grew inside of my body, something I hadn't quite felt or understood before. And I knew that if Kylo even put a scratch on Isabella, I would rip out his throat. The power was growing by the day, my wolf on edge and my body radiating in force.

It was only a matter of time before everything blew up.

CHAPTER 29

ISABELLA

Two hours later, Kylo and I sat at a restaurant inside his pack. I hadn't made a move toward him, hadn't had the confidence to get much closer. The earlier times I had come face-to-face with Kylo, my wolf had made it easy to flirt with him. She always wanted him—always. But now, I could barely feel her on the surface. Ever since we'd left Roman, she had been so distant as if something wasn't right.

But hell, even I couldn't tell anymore with her. My wolf had the raging emotions of a goddess at times, yet could also conceal them too well sometimes.

Across from me, Kylo sipped a glass of red wine and gazed at me, surprisingly calmer than I'd thought he'd be, knowing that I was *supposedly* holding Roman's baby inside of me. I thought that if he was Dolus, he'd at least pick up on the deception since deception *was* Dolus's forte.

But maybe he was hiding it too well.

The restaurant doors opened, and Oliver and Naomi walked into the room with Roger, Kylo's beta.

Kylo glanced over at them and leaned forward. "Did you put them on a mission here?"

"No," I lied, furrowing my brows at the couple that I'd defi-nitely sent on a mission here. "I sent them out on a mission to retrieve some information in Scarlett's pack with the others. Roger was working that way today, wasn't he?"

Kylo nodded and sipped his wine again. "Yes."

"Maybe they met there."

"Maybe."

Not wanting to maintain eye contact with Kylo, I stared a bit harder at Roger, Naomi, and Oliver, my lips curling into a smile. "Whatever they're up to, Roger seems into it." I glanced over at Kylo, hoping to lighten the mood, and winked. "Two strapping men taking Naomi to bed. Who does that sound like?"

For the first time tonight, Kylo chuckled, his taut shoulders relaxing. "I wonder …"

"Sounds fun." I beamed at him and tilted toward him slightly. "I know that I had fun with you and Roman when we were all on good terms."

After falling into a comfortable silence, I sipped some water and cut my steak.

"How far along are you?" Kylo asked, intense brown eyes on me.

I gnawed on the inside of my cheek. "I'm not sure yet. I have a doctor's appointment in a couple days."

He gave me a half-smile and moved closer, holding out his hand for me to place mine in, which I had to do to please him. He intertwined our fingers and pulled my hand to his lips, kissing it softly and then inhaling my scent.

"You must be a few weeks at least. Werewolf pups grow faster, but you smell like me."

My eyes widened. "I smell like you?"

"Your pup." Kylo paused. "Is it really Roman's, or is it mine?"

Mouth drying up, I parted my lips to speak, but no words would come out. This whole pregnancy thing was all fake, an act.

I surely wasn't … I surely wasn't really pregnant. Maybe he was doing this to see how I reacted, to see if I'd stumble.

So, I swallowed hard and put the best damn smile I could on my face. "I assumed it was Roman's because we've been together more often than you and I have. We …" My cheeks flushed as I thought back to the last time Kylo and I had been together. "We haven't been together in what seems like a couple weeks at least."

"So, it could be my pup," Kylo clarified.

My stomach tightened into knots, an uneasy feeling sitting heavily inside me. Fuck, this couldn't be real. I couldn't really be pregnant. Roman would've said something to me, right? He … he wouldn't have let me leave with Kylo if his pup was inside of me.

But that look in his eyes earlier had told me that his jealous and possessive act wasn't just an act. There was some truth behind it, and, Goddess, I hoped that I wasn't really pregnant, that Kylo was just making this up.

I glanced at Oliver, Naomi, and Roger at the bar and had the urge to puke. If I was pregnant, I would fucking get sick right here and right now. There was no way, but … I hadn't really used protection ever, especially with Roman. We did it almost every night.

"Use the restroom," I said to Oliver through our mind link.

Oliver tensed, and then a few moments later, he stood. When I saw him enter the men's restroom, I scrambled to my feet and told Kylo that I needed a pee break—a pregnant woman always had to pee, right? Or was that just a myth? Goddess, I didn't even know the first thing about being pregnant.

Once I slipped into the restroom, I found Oliver at the sinks, washing his hands.

He gazed at me through the mirror, his brows furrowed together. "What's wrong?" he asked.

I glanced into every stall to make sure that nobody was inside. I couldn't let this information get relayed to Kylo in any freaking way. If I really was pregnant and it was his … he'd kill Roman without a second thought.

"I might be pregnant," I whispered, gnawing on the inside of my cheek. "I need you to … to check. Smell my stomach, tell me if you smell another scent."

Oliver swallowed hard. "Isabella, we're in the middle of a war."

"I know, Oliver," I said, my heart sinking. "I know."

After a couple moments, Oliver knelt in front of me and placed his nose near my stomach, inhaling deeply and then tensing. "Along with your scent, there are two other scents coming from your belly."

"Two?!" I whisper-yelled. "There are two?! What the fuck?!"

"One's Roman's, and the other …" He gulped. "The other is Kylo's."

CHAPTER 30

ROMAN

"*R*oman!" Raj whispered, glancing at me from behind a tree.

We stood on top of the prison that Raj had found underneath the ground.

"Follow my lead. The Lycans will follow shortly after, securing the perimeter."

After Isabella had left with Kylo earlier, I'd had to force myself not to run after them. Goddess, I wanted Isabella to stay safe, and if she was pregnant, I wanted our baby safe too. But as shitty as it fucking was, we needed to protect the werewolf species and put them ahead of all else.

One day, Isabella would carry my pup. And one day, we'd start a real life together without Kylo or anyone else in it. We would finally be drama-free and … happy—something we hadn't really been for a long fucking time.

Once Raj glanced around a couple times, he moved quickly from the trees and toward the prison hatch. When he opened it, I sprinted toward him in hopes of finding Derek. His scent lingered heavily in the air here. Together, we slipped into the room. Raj lit a torch.

I glanced around the prison, the setup almost identical to Kylo's. The other day, when Kylo had taken Isabella and me around his lair to deal with a couple of prisoners, I'd made sure to memorize the layout and burn it into my memory forever. If we ever needed to escape from there, I already knew everything I needed to know.

"Where is his scent coming from?" I asked, sniffing around.

I followed Raj, and we walked into a back room. Raj kicked up a rug to see another hatch that led farther down into the ground and supposedly the prison. He opened it up and glanced down into the darkness, throwing the torch to see how far it would go.

It landed about eight feet down—an easy jump for a wolf.

After glancing at me, Raj sucked in a breath and eased himself down into the hole. He picked the torch up and drifted it around the room to see better. When all was clear, he nodded up to me. "Come on. We don't have much time."

And so, I jumped down into the hole with him and flinched when the thick scent of silver hit me. This silver was so fucking strong that this place couldn't have been created or used for any regular wolf, maybe for a Lycan or a divine wolf or … a goddess.

My stomach twisted into knots, yet I followed Raj through the chambers. Most cells were shut off from the rest, almost similar to solitary confinement cells at prisons in the human world. Still, we needed to find Derek, as his scent was becoming stronger by the moment.

After going through nearly all the cells, we came to the last one. Raj kicked the door open with his heel, the door coming off the hinges but the silver burning through his shoe. Derek sat in the cell with his body bound in silver chains and his lip busted.

I ran over to him, ignoring the pain that shot through my body when I touched the silver and quickly undid his chains. His flesh was melted to the bone, his eyes both swollen shut.

"No, please! Don't hurt me again! Please, don't hurt me!"

"Derek, it's me," I said, hoping to soothe him. "It's Roman."

Derek tensed and then sniffed the air. "Roman," he whispered. "Roman …"

Once I finally undid his cuffs, I tossed him over my shoulder because he didn't look like he could stand up straight, never mind walk.

Raj stood at the door, glancing down the opposite hallway and furrowing his brows. "There is a hidden passageway farther down. We should check it out."

"No!" Derek shouted. "No! We have to leave. She'll be back soon. She'll trap us all in here. We can never come back. Never, Roman. Take me home to Isabella and our pack. If I stay here any longer, I might die from—"

A door creaked open from where we had come from. I tensed. Derek snapped his mouth closed. Raj swallowed hard. I could hear his heart pounding inside his chest.

"It's just a couple of the Lycans," he whispered.

But suddenly, the torch went out.

Fuck. Fuck. Fuck.

A moment later, Derek was snatched from my grasp. At the very last second, I grabbed on to his wrist and pulled him back, but the force was too strong. I was being dragged with him, my feet scraping against the ground.

"Raj!" I shouted. "Fucking help me!"

But … I couldn't even hear Raj's breathing, his heart pounding, or his shoes shuffling on the ground. And I hoped to the Goddess that whoever this was hadn't killed him yet because I didn't think I'd be able to get out of here alone.

Whoever it was pulled us farther and farther and farther, back into the cell, and then flicked on a light.

In the center of the room, a foul-scented, white-haired goddess stood.

She resembled the Moon Goddess.

But it wasn't the Moon Goddess. I was sure of that.

CHAPTER 31

ROMAN

*W*e were screwed.

We were fucking screwed.

I bared my canines at the goddess who definitely wasn't the Moon Goddess and growled, my canines aching to sink into her skin and kill her within a moment. But I had more pressing matters at hand, like removing Derek from the situation as quickly as possible and finding out where the fuck Raj had gone.

Wrapping my arms around Derek's waist, I tugged on him with all my strength, heels digging into the concrete so hard that the bottoms of my feet cut open from the burn. The goddess pulled back harder, and I cursed out loud, pain shooting up from my heels.

"What the fuck are you?" I said between clenched teeth.

"Your goddess, Roman," she said, voice booming throughout the room. "Obey me."

And while I had the urge to obey her, an alpha didn't bow to anyone. So, I stood tall, gathered all my growing strength, and ripped Derek from her arms. With all the force I pulled with, Derek slipped from my arms and smacked against the silver-coated wall behind me, grunting.

"You're no Moon Goddess," I growled, immediately shifting into my wolf to protect Derek at all costs even if that cost was my life. I would do anything for my fucking pack, and that included taking down a fake goddess.

When the woman lunged at me, I leaped in her direction and sank my teeth into her abdomen, cutting her open. While a wolf like me shouldn't have the strength to defeat someone like her, I continued to sink my teeth into her flesh and threw her across the room over and over and over again.

Raj suddenly sprinted back into the room with his shirt shredded to pieces and blood smeared all over his heaving chest. He had the silver chains that Derek had been trapped within in his hands. I didn't know what happened to him, but I didn't have the time to ask. Raj grabbed the doorframe and hurried toward me, grabbing my hips. "Roman, let her go!"

But I couldn't stop. Something had taken ahold of me, a power within that I couldn't shake.

"Roman!"

Growling, I let her blood drip over my snout. But her wounds healed quickly.

"Roman!" Raj growled, hands gripping my fur. He tugged as hard as he could, just like I had with Derek; the only difference was that he couldn't pull me away. All I could feel was rage and power rushing through me. "Let her go! We need to keep her alive! She has information!"

"She doesn't deserve to live," I found myself saying, even in my wolf form—something I hadn't even thought was possible. It shouldn't have been, not for a normal wolf.

"Think about Isabella," Raj shouted. "Your mate is counting on you."

Slowly—very slowly—I came back down to reality and dropped the woman from my teeth. As soon as her pathetic body hit the ground, Raj thrust me away from her, grabbed the silver chains, and wrapped them around every one of her limbs, even her neck.

She shrieked, body thrashing back and forth, tugging on the chains that didn't melt her flesh like it would with a wolf, but began transforming her body into one of a fragile, old woman, her skin wrinkling, spine curving, and eyes caving in.

"What the fuck?" I whispered, heart pounding against my rib cage.

"She's turning into her true form," Raj said, brows furrowed. "She must be."

"Let me go!" the woman screamed. "Now!"

"Tell us who you are, and we'll remove you from the chains," I said.

"Roman," Raj scolded, narrowing his eyes.

"Let me go!"

"Who are you?"

"Apaete," the woman said.

The blood drained from Raj's face, and he gulped. "You're the Goddess of Deceit and Dolus's sister, aren't you?"

Suddenly, she paused and grinned wickedly at him. "Yes, and I'll tell you everything you need to know about him, even how to defeat a worthless piece of shit like him, once you let me out of these awful chains."

CHAPTER 32

ISABELLA

"*T*his doesn't make sense," I said breathlessly to Oliver, pacing around the men's restroom and nearly pissing my pants. "What the actual fuck? Roman and I spent the night with Kylo a couple weeks ago, but he never came inside of me. How can this be?"

Leaning against the countertop, Oliver crossed his arms and shook his head. "Pre-cum?"

I crouched down with my head in my hands, tears threatening to spill from my eyes. "Fuck. Fuck. Fuck. Fuck. Fuck. What the hell are we going to do? What the hell am *I* going to do? If I have twins and Kylo is the father and is … *you know who* …" A tear slipped down my cheek. "We're screwed."

Oliver knelt in front of me and grabbed my chin, staring at me intensely. "Stop crying. You're stronger than that, and you're stronger than him. If he is who we think he is, then you will do what you need to do in order to protect our wolves. You're the leader of the Lycans before you are anything else."

"The leader of the Lycans," I whispered, brushing away the tears.

That title meant that I had to put everyone else before me,

that saving the werewolf species had to be more important to me than being a luna, having a mate, and bearing pups. Because if Dolus took over the world, I would no longer be a luna, would no longer have a mate, and would not ever be having pups.

"You're right," I said, pushing my shoulders back. "As much as I hate to say it."

I hated the thought of finally having pups with Roman, only to realize that if it came between my pups and the world, I would have to fucking save the world. My heart ached, and I knew the Moon Goddess would be disappointed. But this was for her.

My mission was to get answers on that bunker underneath Kylo's prison.

When I returned to the table with my thoughts finally set straight, Kylo wasn't there.

Instead, the waiter stood near his empty seat, pouring me another glass of water. "Alpha Kylo needed to leave for a couple moments. One of the prisoners was acting up. He should be back in ten minutes. He told me to tell you that he apologizes for leaving so abruptly."

"He's at his prison?" I asked, brows furrowed together.

The waiter nodded, and I grabbed all my belongings before running out of the restaurant and toward his pack prison. I needed to get there before he came back out and without him noticing me. This might be the only way that I could get in without him questioning my motives. I had questions that I desperately needed answers to, that I knew nobody wouldn't give me even if I asked nicely.

So, I approached the door and smiled sweetly at the guards. "Is Kylo down there?"

A guard nodded.

"I need to talk to him really quick," I said, hoping that they would grant me access.

"He'll be out in a couple moments."

"Are you refusing access to the woman carrying his pup?" I

asked, my tolerance breaking. Maybe I could actually use this to my advantage as much as I hated the thought of using my pups to save the world.

"You're pregnant?" one said.

I held a hand against my stomach. "If you want to see for yourself, you can smell him."

The guards glanced at each other and then opened the door. I hurried down into the prison and into the same room where I had found that underground hatch last time. Instead of descending down into it, I waited behind the door for Kylo to shuffle around the prison above, growling at a wolf for disobedience.

When he was far enough away from me, I pulled up the rug and opened the hatch, staring down into the darkness. *Fuck.* I didn't know if I wanted to do this. It would be fucking dangerous if he caught me, but I knew that I wouldn't have much more time.

After I jumped down into the hole, I cursed at the stench of silver surrounding me. Praying to the Goddess that Kylo wouldn't find me, I adjusted my gaze to the darkness around me and walked cautiously through the silver chambers.

Damn, there had to be so much silver in here. It couldn't be used for normal wolves.

My stomach twisted into knots, but I continued down the corridor and checked in every confined chamber with silver for clues as to where Derek and the Moon Goddess might be, but I came up empty. Completely empty.

At the very end of the hallway, I stopped at a closed chamber door and blew out a deep breath, listening to shoes shuffling against the prison above me. My breath caught in my throat, pain shooting through my body.

If the Goddess was in here, I … I didn't know what I would do.

I would feel so fucking betrayed—so betrayed.

Kylo had spilled his heart to me so many times. If she was here, then Kylo was Dolus.

And, fuck, I didn't know if I was ready to face that fact yet.

After pushing away my fears, I touched my hand to the silver doorknob, my flesh melting, and tried to push it open. Locked. Then, I stood back, preparing to kick down the door, and struck my foot into the silver, the metal searing through the bottom of my shoe.

The door slammed open, the hinges coming off the frame, and I walked into the chamber, coming face-to-face with the golden eyes of a wolf. And not just any wolf …

It was Scarlett, bound in silver and canines lengthened.

CHAPTER 33

ISABELLA

*S*carlett growled at me and bared her blunt little canine teeth. I stared at her in confusion for a few moments because I didn't know what she was doing here, in these chambers, in wolf form. Sure, she was an absolute bitch, but locking a normal wolf down here was ...

Fucked up.

I hated that bitch, but things weren't adding up.

And why hadn't Kylo told me that he'd caught the one woman who had tried to take Roman away from me? I'd thought for sure, if he caught her, that Kylo would tell me what was going on with her and where she was. We had been looking for her for a long fucking time now, and she had just been lounging around in Kylo's underground prison.

"Can you transform back into your human?" I asked her.

She stared at me for a couple moments, blinking, and then she suddenly calmed down and shook her snout from side to side. The look on her face was one of pure agony. The silver seared into her fur, creating deep red marks that I knew would never truly go away.

"Can you answer my questions?" I said, kneeling down to her level.

I didn't know if this was a good idea, but it was my only hope. I had risked my life coming down here. I needed as many answers as I could get because … if Kylo found me down here, I might be fucked.

Scarlett nodded.

"Did Kylo put you down here?" I asked.

She nodded.

"How long ago?"

She tapped her paw on the ground ten times.

"Ten days?"

She shook her head.

No.

"Ten hours?"

She shook her head again.

No.

"Ten minutes."

Scarlett nodded.

"Ten minutes ago?" I asked more to myself than to her. "Were you upstairs before this?"

Another nod.

I ran my hand through my hair and paced the room, my stomach in tight knots. What the fuck was happening? Why hadn't Roman and I seen Scarlett here before? And where the hell had she been before this?

"Where were you?"

Scarlett pointed her snout to the door and then to the left slightly. I backed away a few feet and glanced out the door to the left, opposite of where I had come from. There didn't seem to be —wait. It looked like there was an underground tunnel of sorts. Something deeper in this prison.

Maybe this one connected to the one that Raj had found.

Which meant … something worse.

"Did you see someone else here?" I asked her.

Scarlett nodded and tapped the ground with her paw, drawing a circle on the cement floor. I furrowed my brows, trying to put it all together. Was she writing someone's name on the cement, telling me something else?

"Who?" I asked again.

She drew her paw in a circle once more.

I blinked a few times, frustrated that I couldn't seem to think straight. My thoughts were cluttered with the pups inside my stomach, Kylo's scent inside of me, Kylo right upstairs, and … and Scarlett in front of me, actually talking to me—sorta.

"What are you doing down here?" someone said from behind me.

Shouting in surprise, I jumped up and held a hand to my chest. Kylo stood, his big body blocking the center of the doorway so I couldn't get by. I swallowed hard and backed up farther into the room until I stood by Scarlett's side.

For some reason, I trusted her more than I trusted him.

"Why do you have an underground prison?" I whispered, hand over my stomach.

Scarlett noticed, smelled my stomach, and widened her eyes, not in rage—like she would've if she still hated me—but in fear. She smelled Kylo's scent inside of me too. And instead of biting the pup right out of my stomach, she stood in front of me and growled at Kylo even though her body was still wrapped in chains.

Kylo growled back at her and stepped toward me, holding out a hand. "You shouldn't be here, not with Scarlett. She'll kill you."

Scarlett growled again, baring her teeth at Kylo, as if to tell him not to take a step closer.

"Why do you have an underground prison?" I asked again, heart pounding.

"To lock up wolves like her." He stepped closer. "Now, come on."

When Kylo touched my hand, Scarlett snapped her canines at Kylo. Kylo grabbed her by the snout and snapped it shut until it cracked. I shivered in response, but Scarlett didn't stop trying to thrust her body between Kylo and me. She glanced back to me and then at the now-open door.

Somehow, someway, I knew what she was telling me to do.

She wanted me to run far, far, far away.

I took a step toward the door, silently thanked Scarlett for this—even though I hated her—and sprinted toward the door, escaping through it at the last moment and running down the hidden tunnel.

Scarlett howled, the sound echoing through the prison, and then her voice suddenly disappeared. My heart ached for her. I had never liked her, and she suddenly turned out to be on my side. Maybe she didn't trust Kylo as much as I thought she did. Maybe I had her wrong all this time. But I would never know now.

When I thought I had made it a good enough distance away from him, Kylo snatched me by the back of my neck and pulled me into the air.

"You're not going anywhere, Isabella. You're mine."

CHAPTER 34

ROMAN

"*L*et me go," Apaete roared. "Now!"

Raj stepped between Apaete and me. "You'll answer our questions now."

"What the hell do you want me to tell you? That Isabella is pregnant with twins?" She grinned wickedly between us, eyes blazing. "Is that what you want me to say to you? Is that the truth you want me to unleash into this world?"

My hands dropped from fists, and I sucked in a breath. "What?"

Isabella is pregnant with twins, and I fucking left her with that bitch Kylo?

I growled under my breath and shook my head, claws digging into my palms again and cutting right through the skin. How could I fucking do that to my mate? She was carrying my pups.

"One of them is yours," Apaete continued. "And the other is Kylo's."

Stomach tightening into knots, I shot forward and grabbed her by the throat, claws sinking into her skin enough to draw blood from her immortal body. She might live forever, her wounds might heal at lightning speed, but this still felt good.

"Roman," Raj warned.

Apaete laughed menacingly.

"Those are my pups," I said.

"Is that what you think? Have you smelled her belly lately?"

Another boisterous growl escaped my lips.

"Roman! Stop it," Raj said again. Once he finally pulled me back from her, he placed a hand on the center of my chest and shoved me toward the door. "She's trying to deceive you. Don't believe her." He turned back to her. "What else do you know?" Raj growled, showing his canines. "Tell us."

When she didn't say anything, he tightened the chains, so they burned even more into her skin.

Apaete yowled out and shook her head. "Fine! If the human's spirit is weak enough, Dolus can take hold of any human." Apaete ground her teeth together, skin scorching to the bone. "Now, would you let me go? Now! I can't deal with this searing pain anymore."

With rage rushing through me, I hit Apaete right across the face and dislocated her jaw. I never hit women, but, fuck, this chick was a goddess who had been fucking with us for the past few months, if not years now.

Raj cleared his throat and pulled me back. "You're not finished answering our questions."

"What else do you want me to say?" Apaete asked.

"Why hasn't Dolus come to face us?" Raj said. "What's holding him back?"

"Dolus is afraid of you," Apaete said to me.

I glanced over at Raj to see if he thought she was lying because, apparently, I couldn't tell the difference. For me, she was too fucking good at lying through her teeth, but maybe I was too hyped up on adrenaline and could think of nothing but ripping her to pieces.

Raj nodded, as if to say she was telling the truth.

"Why?" I asked, jaw clenched.

"Because you're stronger than he is and you have the woman he loves. He's always lived in your shadow since the beginning of wolf, the beginning of man, and the beginning of gods."

"You're lying," I said.

"Untie me, and I'll prove it to you," Apaete said.

Raj and I stared at each other for a couple moments.

Derek stood behind her, shaking his head with tears flowing down his cheeks. "Don't do it. She's fucking with you both. If you let her go, she's going to chain us all."

After a couple moments, Raj's eyes glazed over, as if he was talking through the mind link to the Lycans above us. The hatch opened down the corridor, and the sound of claws scraping against the ground drifted through my ears. Raj wanted to release her. He saw something inside of her that I couldn't.

He easily saw through her lies.

When the Lycans were surrounding our room and guarding all the exits, Raj nodded to me. "Let's release her for a couple moments. I want to see what kind of information she has. She knows Dolus better than all of us."

"You will release me, and if I give you the information you need, you will let me go."

Raj glanced at me again, jaw twitching, and then nodded. "Sure."

"Sure?!" Derek shouted. "She tortured me in this chamber for days! She tried to break me. She made me into her... her toy to haunt Isabella and everyone else!"

I growled at him to snap his mouth closed. I wouldn't let this goddess go, no matter what, but we needed this information. If she gave us something good, we would lock her back up and use the information to do what we had to do. If she didn't, then we would torture the living divineness out of her until she did.

"Do it," I growled, "before I regret it."

Raj walked forward and unlocked her cuffs, stepping back as

136

quickly as he could. His nails lengthened into claws behind his back in case she tried to kill us in a single instant. "Talk," Raj demanded.

The goddess grew back into her younger self—a woman who didn't look like the Moon Goddess anymore—with blazing purple eyes and raven-colored hair. She straightened her back and lifted a hand toward me. "Dolus had your mother killed in a rogue attack, Roman, and then had me put a spell on you, so you couldn't recognize who you truly were."

"And who the fuck am I to you?" I said, anger growing within me.

I hated talking about my mother, especially when someone else brought them up, and I hated this asshole goddess who'd had to be released to apparently show me who I was really without whatever spell that she put on me.

A couple moments later, with her finger still pointed in my direction, I felt the urge to shift. My head felt heavy, a searing pain shooting through it, and my nails lengthened into claws. I growled and tried desperately to fight it, but I couldn't …

I transformed into my beast, but something felt off.

"Oh, Goddess," Raj whispered underneath his breath, stepping away from me in disbelief with wide eyes. He stared at me, brows furrowing together, a hundred emotions flooding his eyes. "Isabella is in trouble."

"That's what you fucking see?" I asked through clenched canines. "What's wrong with me?"

Raj shook his head and ran a hand through his thick black hair. "Roman, you're more than a wolf, more than just an alpha. You're one of the first wolves. I've been reading up on them lately, and you… you fit the description. Your entire story fits the description. You … you have to be one of the first. And Isabella … she's in big trouble. We left her in the hands of a liar."

Apaete lifted her hand to the door behind Raj, and suddenly, it slammed shut, trapping us in the room with her. She stalked closer to us with a smile so sinister that it scared the living hell out of me. "There is a part of the divine wolves' story that you don't know about, lost through the ages." She stepped closer to me. "There weren't two divine wolves. There were three."

CHAPTER 35

ROMAN

Three divine wolves. Three?!
I stood back in shock and swallowed hard. It would explain so much yet so little. Was that why Kylo and I felt equally attracted to Isabella? But why hadn't I known about this before? Why was this the first time I was finding out?

My hands balled into fists, and I growled through my teeth.

Like I'd promised Derek, I wouldn't let her walk out of here alive. I would torture her for everything that she had done to Derek, to Isabella, and to my relationship with Isabella. This woman had made Isabella believe that Kylo was the only person in this world for her, and I could never forgive any goddess for that.

Not even the Moon Goddess.

"We will lock her back up," I said through gritted teeth.

Apaete widened her eyes and shot forward, baring her teeth. She wrapped a hand around my throat and pinned me against the wall, squeezing as tightly as she could, as if she wanted to murder me right then and there.

"We had a deal!" she screamed.

With that power within me, I shoved her off me with ease.

She stumbled back until she hit the silver chains and fell to her knees from the sheer amount of pain she must've been in. As she screamed out, I latched the chains around her wrists and ankles, ignoring the pain as I secured her to this prison.

"What are you doing?" Raj asked tensely behind me.

Grabbing Derek, I lifted him to his feet and opened the door for him to escape. I was sure that he wanted to get out of here as soon as humanly possible because I wouldn't want to be anywhere that I had been tortured for weeks.

"Get him away and to safety," I ordered one of the Lycans. "Bring him back to your packhouse. Make sure nobody takes him again, or I'll have Isabella on your ass about it. This is her best friend."

Two Lycans accompanied Derek out of the prison, taking him home. I ordered them to keep him safe and secure until this was all over, then I would let my dear Isabella see him again. They deserved a reunion that they both remembered forever.

I turned back to Apaete and punched her square in the mouth, watching the blood trickle down her chin. Unable to stop myself, I hit her again and again and again, each punch more forceful, anger rushing through me. Not only was she now spewing lies, but she had also tortured the shit out of my packmate.

She deserved this.

To my surprise, Raj stood back and watched, not stopping me once.

When her head hung low and she couldn't find the energy to lift it anymore, I marched out of the door and growled to myself. I would be back tomorrow to make her life a living fucking hell, day and night.

"Where the hell are you going?" Raj said, hurrying after me once he secured the prison.

"You said it yourself," I said to Raj, storming down the hallway and leaping out of the hatch in the prison. I stepped onto concrete and continued toward the exit, needing and aching to find Isabella to make sure she was safe. "Isabella is in danger with Kylo."

"If there really is a third divine wolf, then this changes everything," Raj said.

I stopped walking in the middle of the woods and grabbed his shoulder, shaking my head. "Do you really believe anything that she said? She's Dolus's sister and the damn Goddess of Deceit. She made Isabella believe that she was the Moon Goddess, Raj."

"But—"

"Put Isabella aside. She disrespected *our* Moon Goddess, and she must know where she is. If that doesn't scream danger to you, I don't know what does." I sighed and glanced through the trees. "I'm going to find Isabella to make sure she's safe. She's carrying my pups. You get as much information out of this woman as you can."

I didn't know if what the goddess had said was true. I didn't know if I was the third divine wolf or just a man with powers far too great for this world. But what I did know was that I needed to make sure that my Isabella was okay. There was no way that I'd let that bastard take her and my children from me.

No fucking way.

Isabella was mine.

CHAPTER 36

ISABELLA

K ylo hiked me over his shoulder and walked with me down the hallway, passing Scarlett's cell. Inside, her remains were scattered on the floor atop a river of her blood, her foul scent dissipating slowly. My stomach turned, knots forming, and my hormonal ass had the urge to cry out for her.

She had been the one to get under my skin with Roman, but she'd tried to save me from Kylo.

"Let me go!" I shouted at Kylo, kicking and punching and kneeing him in any way possible, but his grip on me tightened so hard until I couldn't move, not even wiggle around in the slightest. "Let me go, Kylo, now!"

"You're running away from me," he said, body tense. "No."

"If you don't let me go, then I can't trust you."

But I didn't trust him anyway, and he already knew that. I had run away from him after Scarlett tried to protect me. I thought that he was the foulest man alive and couldn't fathom how I could be holding his baby. Honestly, I didn't think it was true. It couldn't be.

After easily leaping through the hatch, like he had some sort of godly powers, Kylo landed on the concrete ground above and walked with me toward an empty cell. "You shouldn't have even been down there in the first place."

"Why were you keeping it a secret?!" I cried, fidgeting in his grasp.

"Because you didn't need to know about it."

"I'm supposed to be your divine mate! I should know about a prison you keep underneath your pack. I shouldn't have to figure it out for myself and find Scarlett locked away. You didn't even tell me that you had her here!"

"I just found her."

"Don't give me that shit!"

Kylo walked into an empty cell. "I'm not lying to you, Isabella. Stop talking back to me."

"No!" I shouted again, anger rushing through me. "First, you kept your information on Scarlett from me. Next, you killed Scarlett and snatched me. Now, you're about to lock me in a cage so that I stay as yours and aren't away from you!"

In the midst of my insanity, I tried hard to move around him, to get the fuck out of here, to leave this pack prison and property and find Roman. I didn't belong here, and Kylo was fucking mad —so fucking deranged.

But that was how I felt too now.

When Kylo successfully locked the cell on me, I screamed, "Let me out!"

He stood outside the bars with his arms crossed and sorrow in his eyes. "I'm sorry that it's come to this."

"I don't believe a word that comes out of your mouth," I snapped. "And I really don't believe that I'm holding your pup inside of me. You don't fucking deserve it! You're crazy for locking up your own mate, crazy for killing Scarlett, and crazy for everything you've fucking done."

Kylo clenched his jaw, brown eyes softening even more. And if I wasn't screaming at him, I would've sorta, kinda felt sorry for him. He looked like he was breaking on the inside, that he truthfully hated every word that had come out of my mouth.

"I'll show you that it's true," Kylo said, turning on his heel and disappearing down the hall.

I placed a hand against my stomach and inhaled deeply, calming my racing heart. And Oliver might've smelt two distinct scents inside of my stomach—one from Kylo and one from Roman—I couldn't seem to smell it anymore. The aroma only happened when Kylo was near.

My stomach tightened.

A heartbeat.

Only one.

Not two. One.

A couple moments later, he reappeared with a female doctor who I'd met only once before. She smiled at me and explained how she usually delivered pack pups and how she wanted to check up on mine.

I looked between Kylo and her and stepped closer to the cell door. Instead of walking in with me—Kylo must've thought that I would hurt her, and I fucking would've—she reached through the cell bars and gently touched my stomach, placing an enhanced stethoscope for wolf use only against my bare belly.

She glanced at me and then at Kylo, giving us a small smile. "There are two heartbeats. One is faint, the other strong."

Kylo stood back against the wall with his brows furrowed together in a hurt stare and grimaced at her, barely looking up at me. "You're dismissed."

The woman scurried back down the hallway and disappeared through the prison doors.

"What did you do to me?" I asked.

"I didn't do anything to you, Isabella. You were trying to run away from me."

"You're a liar! I don't have two pups inside of me." I seethed, anger rushing through me. I gripped the bars on the cell, no

144

matter how much they stung my palms, and glared at him through the cell. "You're a fucking liar!"

Thousands of thoughts ran through my mind at lightning speed. Trapped in this cell, I believed that Kylo was right and that I was going crazy—and not because of him, but because of me. That was what I wanted to think, but I knew it wasn't true.

Dolus was making me crazy.

I dug my claws into the silver to ground myself, the searing pain shooting up my claws. I whimpered but continued to hold on because I feared that I'd crumble under the pressure of keeping my baby safe, hoping that Roman hadn't gotten himself killed already and praying that Kylo wasn't Dolus the second I let go of the silver, of the pain.

"You need to let me go," I whispered. "Please, Dolus."

When I said that damn god's name, Kylo's strong gaze faltered for a moment. But in that moment, everything felt so real, everything felt like I was right, that this wasn't a big story that I'd fabricated in my head.

My body felt so weak, but I found the energy to reach through the bars and cup his face. Kylo placed his large hand over mine, fingers between mine, and squeezed tightly, like he didn't want to let go, like he wanted to be mine forever.

"I can't do this anymore," I whispered, pain shooting through my body. "I can't do this for a thousand more lifetimes. Please, stop chasing me. Roman is the only person that I will love until I die. I cannot love you in this life, Dolus. I can't."

CHAPTER 37

KYLO

*D*ark circles around her eyes, trembling lips, and annoyance in her every word, Isabella seethed at me with so much spite, hatred, and sadness. I stared at her from outside the cell, suddenly realizing everything that I had done to her and Roman. These past few weeks, I had done whatever I had to do to keep her safe.

I knew that I had.

But then why had I put her into a cell, locked her up, and forced her to stand inside a silver cage? My heart broke as I stared at her big eyes, filled with tears. She shouldn't be in here, and *I* was the one who had trapped—*forced*—her.

"Dolus," Isabella whispered.

"I'm not Dolus," I said, heart shattering even more. "I'm Kylo."

Isabella stared at me and shook her head, as if she didn't believe a word that I said. She didn't believe that all I wanted to do was protect her from the darkness that was inside everyone, even Roman and myself. We might've spent lifetimes together, but I never thought that the other half of me—the other divine wolf—would hate me as much as she did.

"You're a terrible liar."

"I'm not lying," I whispered, desperate for her to believe me. I stepped closer to her with my brows furrowed. "I swear to you, Isabella, I'm Kylo and nobody else. I remember everything about us from the very start."

I placed my hand on the silver cage bars and let it burn my skin. I wanted to show her that I was willing to do anything for her. It was all I had wanted this entire time since I'd met her, but Isabella hadn't wanted it from the start.

It wasn't my fault that Isabella's wolf and my wolf were mated.

It wasn't my fault that I wanted him to be happy for once after what Scarlett had done to us.

It wasn't my fault that I had been falling in love with Isabella for weeks now.

No matter how hard I tried, I couldn't stop this feeling inside of me. Nothing I did to protect her seemed to matter to her or Roman anymore. She hated me more and more and more every day, and the thought of my second mate hating me killed me on the inside.

I didn't want to live like this anymore.

I couldn't.

"The night at the lake with the Moon Goddess …"

After closing my eyes, I thought back to that weekend and how good I'd felt after just a single night with her. We didn't even do anything together, just lay under the stars and spent time with each other. Nothing else had happened.

"That Moon Goddess wasn't real," Isabella said.

"Yes, she was. That night was real."

"No, it wasn't."

My throat closed up, and my stomach twisted into knots. "The Moon Goddess was real, Isabella. How do you not believe that she was there? We talked to her, laughed with her, and took orders from her."

Isabella glared at me. "You're full of shit, Dolus. I'm not stupid."

"You're not stupid, Isabella," I whispered.

I hated how she didn't believe that it was me, really me.

"Just leave me alone!" Isabella shouted, tears pouring down her cheeks now. She moved into the corner of the cell, farthest away from me, and shook her head. "Please, let me be. I don't want to be with you, Dolus."

Knowing that I would never get through to Isabella like this, I sighed and stepped back from the silver cage. My Isabella didn't believe me; she refused to believe anything that I was saying, and I couldn't understand why she hated me.

"Go!" she shouted.

Leaving Isabella in the cell, I walked deeper into the prison and toward the one place where I kept the thing that could destroy us both. I tapped the code into the lock and pulled open the door. Locked away in another glass case, the flower shimmered under the light.

That fucking flower.

Very carefully, I unlocked the glass case and took out the flower. The petals and leaves seemed to grow more vibrant and alive the second I took it out. It burned my skin, melting it away almost as quickly as the silver had downstairs in the lower prison.

If I broke away a piece, crushed it into small flakes, sprinkled it inside a glass, it would dissipate into the water and become a liquid lethal enough to kill Isabella or … *me*. Isabella thought I was Dolus, Roman thought I was Dolus, and I … I just thought I was me.

But things had been changing and happening that I couldn't explain.

Not in the fucking slightest.

Worst-case scenario: Dolus was inside of me, so this would

kill him too. I broke a piece, crushed it between my fingers, and sprinkled it into a glass of water. I placed the glass to my lips. If this was what I had to do, that was what I would do. I would do anything to protect Isabella from the darkness … even if the darkness was me.

CHAPTER 38

ROMAN

"You're not allowed in here," one of Kylo's prison guards said when I approached the doors.

I had snuck onto Kylo's property—because nobody would willingly allow me inside—and followed Isabella's scent all over the land until I came to the prison. If she had gone down into the underground chambers, I didn't know if I would be able to get her out alive.

Especially if Kylo was down there with her.

"Let me through," I said between gritted teeth. "My mate is down there."

"Alpha Kylo has given strict orders not to let anyone down into the prison."

Snatching both guards by their throats, I slammed them against the door and lifted them into the air, squeezing so tightly that they couldn't breathe. "You either give me access to the prison or I take it after I take your lives. Choose fucking wisely."

After struggling to get out of my hold—and failing—they looked at each other and nodded. I dropped them and watched them stumble to their knees, the skin on their knees ripping at the impact. Once they staggered to their feet, one took a key out of his pocket and thrust it into the lock.

The door swung open, the foul scent of Kylo drifting outside. I stepped into the prison and grabbed the door, glancing over my shoulder at the two men.

"Don't tell Kylo that I was here or else I'll kill his pup growing in my mate's stomach."

As if they knew what I was talking about, the two quickly nodded. I balled my hands into fists and shut the door quietly behind me. I didn't believe for a second that Isabella was carrying Kylo's pup, but if it kept them quiet, then I'd use it.

After silently descending the steps, I followed Isabella's scent to a cell, where she was curled up in the corner with her head in her hands, soft whimpers coming from her.

I hurried toward the cage and wiggled the cell. "Isabella."

Her head snapped up, gaze falling on me. So many emotions crossed her face, finally landing on fear. "Roman, what are you doing here?" she whispered, eyes growing wide. "You can't be here. He'll lock you up too."

"Where is he?" I asked, rage rushing through me.

Tears welled up in her eyes as she stared at me. She moved closer to the bars and placed her hands over mine. "I'm sorry," she whispered, covering her mouth to muffle a sob. "I'm so sorry."

"What are you sorry for? What's going on?"

"I … there's …" More tears flowed down her cheeks. "I'm carrying Kylo's pup."

I sucked in a sharp breath. Had that goddess told the truth? Or was this all Dolus's thoughts, getting in both our heads, fucking with our minds? I didn't know if Isabella really was carrying both our pups or not.

But all I cared about now was getting Isabella out of here. If she had both our pups inside of her, then we'd deal with that fucker later. Isabella needed to be safe before she could have any pups.

"It doesn't matter." It did.

"Roman, you need to leave …"

I turned around and searched for some keys, anything to get Isabella out of this fucking cell. She was a sobbing mess right now and couldn't think straight. Hell, neither could I, but I wouldn't let Isabella die here, in this prison.

When I searched everywhere and found nothing, I placed my hands upon the silver bars once more and used all my strength. The metal burned right through the skin on my hands, but I didn't care. I pulled the bars apart as far as I could until they bent enough for Isabella to walk through.

She stared at me from inside the cell with wide eyes. "Roman, wh-what happened to you?"

"There are three divine wolves, Isabella," I said to her, not knowing how else to explain this newfound power inside of me. I grabbed her hand and pulled her from the cell. "Now, come on. We have to get you out of here. Now."

Something broke farther down the hallway. I gripped Isabella tightly and pulled her in the opposite direction. But the sound of quick footsteps followed the crash, walking toward us swiftly. Isabella pulled me into a room with an open hatchet.

"We won't make it out of the prison without Kylo finding us. If we can get him down here, then we can lock him up and see if he's really Dolus or not," Isabella whispered, gesturing down the hatchet. "There are silver cages down there."

Just like there were at the other prison.

"And an underground tunnel."

An underground tunnel that Isabella could use to escape.

"Okay," I whispered, glancing over my shoulder toward the door. The footsteps became louder and louder and louder, and then I heard Kylo growl. Knowing that we didn't have much more time, I took Isabella's face in my hands and kissed her on the lips. "I love you so much."

Taken aback, Isabella smiled. "I love you too."

My stomach twisted, and I pushed her toward the hatch. When she stuck her body into it and jumped down into the darkness, I smiled down at her and slammed the door closed, locking it from up above.

"Roman!" she shouted through the mind link. *"What are you doing?! Get down here now!"*

"Run, Isabella. Don't look back."

"But, Roman—"

"I'm saving our future." I paused and turned toward the door, drawing my claws and shifting into my wolf. *"You and our pups are our future. If I don't survive today, know that I will always be with you."*

CHAPTER 39

ISABELLA

"*R*oman!" I screamed at the top of my lungs, hoping that he would hear the desperation in my voice and open this hatch, so I could leap out of here and help him fight Kylo because I couldn't fucking lose him.

I didn't care if Kylo had been my mate for thousands of years. Roman was my mate now. And as much as I fucking hated thinking this, they both could be the fathers to my pups. What kind of fucked up world would it be if they both died because Roman had locked me down here?

Squatting down, I eyed the top of the silver hatch and leaped into the air until my hands reached it. In the couple moments that I hovered in the air, I shoved my hand against the hatch and burned it, nearly down to the bone, and then landed back on my feet, stumbling into the silver wall.

"Roman!" I screamed. I whimpered and glared up at the door with tears in my eyes. "Let me out now!"

I jumped at the hatch again.

And again.

And again.

Until my hands bled and the wounds wouldn't close up

anymore. I placed the burning flesh on my knees and doubled over, tears racing from my cheeks, an unexplainable pain in my heart suffocating me.

I couldn't lose him.

My wolf whimpered.

But right now, I couldn't deal with that unaffected bitch telling me that I needed Kylo. Kylo had done nothing but hurt us. He'd locked us in that cage only a couple moments ago, blamed Roman over and over for his mistakes, and even tried to convince me that Roman had cheated on me.

How could I …

"Because we love Kylo," my wolf said to me.

Her voice drifted through my ears from one side to the other, the sound so serene that it was almost calming. It was almost divine and angelic. And if I remembered one thing from my childhood—hell, from just before I'd turned eighteen—it was that my wolf wasn't an angel.

She was a brat.

And she only liked Roman.

So what the fuck was inside me, desperately trying to get me to love Kylo again? What was pushing and pulling me? What was slowly trying to take control of my body? Maybe … just maybe, it was Dolus. Or something worse.

Slams and rumbles echoed through the hatch from above, pulling me out of my thoughts. I stared up at the silver door, my hands still bleeding and trembling. There was no way in hell that I'd be able to get out through there, and there was no way in hell that they both wouldn't die if I didn't try to stop them soon.

I turned around toward the cells and hurried down the hallway, pushing against whatever was inside of me, begging me to stay. Whatever it was, was damn tough because I literally had to pick up each foot and slam it back on the ground, like trudging through thick mud.

While the silver chambers were all shut, except the one that

Scarlett's body was in, there was one door, one tunnel, into the darkness. I stared into the endless pit of black, not able to see twenty feet ahead of me, even with my enhanced eyesight.

"Fuck," I whispered, squeezing my eyes closed and shaking my head. "I have to do this."

But I didn't want to because all I could hear were howls and whimpers upstairs. My mate and my divine mate were fighting to the death, desperately trying to kill each other for me and for no good reason at all.

No matter what, I had to obey Roman's wishes. I had asked him to believe in me for months and begged him to see me as his equal. And now, it was my turn. Roman might be as strong as me, but I had been trying to keep him out of my Lycan business as much as possible.

Now, I had to believe that he'd do the right thing.

This was how everything would end.

If Kylo was Dolus, then I would have to survive. I wouldn't survive, waiting down here.

I ran my hand over my stomach and felt the heartbeat of my babies. Whatever happened upstairs or in the days to come, I would make sure that my pups knew who their fathers were— one an evil man and the other a savior.

CHAPTER 40

KYLO

With inhuman strength, Roman threw me against the silver cell bars. My body hit with a thud, skin sizzling at the mere contact of metal on wolf flesh. Before he could run at me again, I found myself standing back up and growling at him.

Five minutes ago, I'd stood in one of the cells with the flower in my hands, about to end this all. I had been so close—so fucking close to ceasing this madness once and for all. But when I'd smelled Roman slithering his way into my prison, I couldn't stop myself from running out here, aching to kill him.

I had lost all control, and I couldn't regain it.

No matter how hard I tried, a power inside me had forced me to drop the flower and stalk through the prison, wanting to rip Roman to shreds. And for the first time, I feared that it really was Dolus because it didn't make sense.

Whenever I was with Isabella, I was calm—unless she was running away from me.

Hell, when she was in that cage, I had come back down to earth so fucking quickly that I was going to kill myself for her—fucking kill myself. And maybe I should've when I had the chance because I couldn't kill Roman. Not only was he so much stronger now, but he was also my oldest friend.

"Roman," I said through clenched teeth, tensing so I could control myself.

But Roman saw that as a threat, and he lunged at me, wrapped his rough hand around my throat, turned me around, and shoved me back against the jail cell. When I hit, my body sizzled again. I winced and bit my tongue, thrusting myself off the bars and twirling around to meet him face-to-face.

Rage rushing through me, power overtaking my body, I pounced back at him and knocked my hands against his chest, sending him backward and against the wall. The cement cracked from the force, yet Roman didn't even look impacted.

"Kill him for me," Isabella said through the mind link. *"We can be together forever, my love."*

I squeezed my eyes closed, knowing that she didn't really want this. She loved Roman, more than she had ever or would ever love me. I was just hopelessly waiting for a woman who could never love me.

"No," I said back to her. *"I won't kill him."*

But my body reacted to her words almost naturally, rushing back at Roman before he had the chance to jump at me. I drove my fist into the side of his face, using all the force I could gather, pushing him back into the wall.

"Don't worry about me, Kylo," she said softly through my head. *"I will love you, no matter what happens. I just want to be with you again. One night with you will never be enough. I ache for eternity."*

"Stop!" I shouted, slamming my fist back into Roman's face. "Stop it now!"

ROMAN

"Kill him, Roman," Isabella said through the mind link. *"We can be together forever, my love. I know you want to eliminate him from this*

world. I know how much anger you have built up inside of you, how much pain you have from your mother's death."

I pummeled my fists into Kylo and thrust him off me, stalking toward him and pushing him farther and farther back toward the wall. I clenched my jaw and used Isabella's words to fuel myself. If Kylo had been a good friend, he would've been there that day to help stop my mom from dying a horrible death from the rogues.

But he was never my friend. He was always my enemy, always Dolus.

"He thinks your mom deserved to die. He thinks she was a weak bitch, someone his father could take advantage of, just like Kylo tried to take advantage of me," Isabella said through my head again. *"Why have you let someone like that live for all these weeks? You should be ashamed of yourself for letting this go on for so long."*

"What are you saying?" I asked through the mind link, kicking Kylo in the gut. *"I didn't kill him because you didn't want me to. You told me that you thought you loved him. All I ever wanted was to see you happy."*

"Then, kill him!" she said. *"That will make me happy. I want his head. Then, I will submit to you for eternity. This is the only way."*

Anger rushed through me. *This isn't Isabella.*

"Isabella would never submit to me," I said back. *"She's a brat."*

My brat.

At the same time, Kylo and I both threw a right hook at each other and shouted, "Get out of my fucking head!"

And in that instant, we both stopped fighting and stood back from each other, breathing hard and seething. But we weren't angry with the other—at least, I wasn't angry with him now. I was trying my hardest not to run at him and lose control.

This was Dolus's doing.

This was him controlling us.

He wanted us to be weak. He wanted us to be drowning in so much anger for each other that we couldn't think straight. He wanted us to destroy each other, so *he* could be the one to be with Isabella. This wasn't a fight against Kylo anymore.

This was a fight against Dolus.

"We're being controlled," I said through gritted teeth, muscles swelling so much that I thought that they'd burst out of my fucking skin. I clenched my fists even harder by my sides, building up power in each of them, terrified that if I let one go against Kylo, I'd kill him.

"Leave," Kylo said. "Before I kill you. You have to leave."

And though I wanted to leave, I couldn't move from the spot.

"I can't move," I said.

"Then, we stay like this until Isabella comes back," he said, entire body tense.

"I trapped her down in the hatch. She's not getting out."

"There's an underground tunnel. She'll find her way out. She'll stop this. Believe in her."

CHAPTER 41

"*Give in, Roman,*" Isabella said through my mind for the fiftieth time in the past twenty minutes. "*Give up control, and we can be together forever.*"

"*I will never let you control me.*"

"*No matter what, Roman ...*" she said in my head, the voice turning deep and manly.

Dolus. This was really him.

"*I will break you down to pieces and kill you. I will see my first love again. There is no way that you can live any longer. You've gotten in the way for far too long, and your will won't break, so I must get rid of you. If you had succumbed to the pressure, then you wouldn't have to die. But ... it's too late. I have broken Kylo's will down. The last bit will be easy to take, so I can become him.*"

"Kylo," I shouted, sweat pouring down my back, "resist him."

Kylo snapped his head to the side, his eyes shifting between gold and an obsidian black, his lips twitching and his veins bulging from his skin. No matter how hard I tried, I wouldn't be able to save him.

"Don't let him take control of you," I screamed at him. "Think of Isabella!"

I hated using Isabella to calm him down, but this was the only way I could think of getting him to settle, to stay calm, to not lose this war to the monster who had been trying to break us both down from the start.

He had always been physically stronger than me, but right now, his will to live was breaking. And I knew that if we fought right here and now, Kylo would win. He might not be mentally strong, but with a god's strength, he would kill me. I might've thought to have a god's strength too, but Kylo had *always* been stronger.

"It's no use," Dolus said through my mind. "There is no saving him."

"Yes," I said back to him. "There is saving him. You don't have control of him yet."

Though by the way Kylo squeezed his eyes closed and the vein twitched in his neck, I could tell that he was losing the battle, that he was moments away from giving up control and surrendering to Dolus—the man we'd both vowed to kill in order to protect Isabella.

"You promised to kill Dolus!" I shouted at him, heart pounding in my chest. "Don't let him control you. Don't fucking let him harm you because once he has you, he'll have Isabella too. And your pup and everything that you've worked so hard for! Don't let go!"

My voice was hoarse as I continued screaming at him to be stronger than me, like he always was. Because, while I hated the man, I hated Dolus for doing this to all of us even more. I wanted to kill that man myself.

"Say good-bye, Roman," Dolus said in my mind, accompanied with the images of Isabella running aimlessly through the dark underground tunnels to nothingness. Tears streamed down her face, and her lips parted in despair as she cried out my name. "This is our last chance to be together forever, and I'm not going to let it slip past me."

Every fucking moment that I'd spent with Isabella flashed through my mind. Every fucking hope and dream and wish for the future made me ache in pain. I refused to leave Isabella with Dolus. I refused to die. I would be the one to stop this and pull Kylo out of the darkness.

I would not fall to a man who couldn't even materialize, who used other people's bodies for his own. I would not fall to a weak god who seemed to be losing his power. I would rip him to pieces if he came at me again.

KYLO

"You're nothing," Isabella said into my ear. *"You're nobody."*

"Stop it," I whispered to myself, squeezing my eyes tightly together and shaking my head. Isabella's voice was so loud in my head that I couldn't think straight. I knew it wasn't her, but that didn't mean my body knew that. "Please, stop it."

"Kylo!" Roman shouted, but his voice was drowned out by Isabella's.

"You're worthless. You couldn't even keep your mate with you. You would never be able to keep me too, without killing Roman. Roman will take me away from you every single time. Kill him for me, Kylo. Please, lose control."

"Stop listening to that voice!" Roman shouted over the sounds. "It's Dolus."

"If I give up control," I said back to the voice, *"you'll have Isabella until the day you die."*

"We'll have Isabella until we die," the voice said, finally becoming deeper until it wasn't Isabella's voice anymore, but Dolus's, sounding the same way it had when he took control of Scarlett.

My body ached, losing the fight. I wouldn't be able to keep this up much longer.

No matter how strong I claimed to be, I was nothing.

"Don't give up, Roman," I said between clenched teeth, my canines growing. "Don't give in to me. Stay strong."

"Don't fucking say that, Kylo," he said, body trembling. "You're not going to lose control."

But I had already lost control. I only had a couple more moments of free will left. And I knew what I had to do to end this madness forever. If Dolus took control of me, I wouldn't be able to use my body anymore. I wouldn't be me.

"The flower," I said before I lost complete control of my entire shaking body. "It's three doors down, crushed up in a glass of water. Make sure Isabella doesn't use it. Tell her … tell her to give it to me."

And those were the last words I could force past my lips before Dolus took control and coerced me to sprint at Roman, Isabella's first and only true lover and one of my oldest fucking friends. I doubted that I would ever see that man again.

CHAPTER 42

ISABELLA

*urn around."*
"*Go back."*
"*Stop running."*

I pushed the tears off my cheeks and ran faster through the dark tunnels, not knowing where I was going but knowing that I needed to find an exit as soon as possible. The voice inside my head only made me move faster despite wanting to slow me down.

When I didn't stop, my feet suddenly became heavier, as if whatever was trapped inside of me couldn't get me to mentally break so it had to resort to being physical with me now. And I fucking refused to let that happen.

Instead of letting it stop me, I picked up my feet and trudged forward, keeping my eyes on the smallest light at the end of the tunnel. I had something to look forward to, something to keep me moving.

If I didn't get back to Kylo's prison soon, then Roman and Kylo were going to kill each other. I would lose my mate for good, and my pups would lose their damn fathers. I couldn't and wouldn't allow something like that to happen.

The closer I ran toward the light, the heavier my feet became.

"Someone!" I shouted through the darkness. "Is anyone there?"

"Isabella?" someone asked, a silhouette appearing before the light. "Is that you?"

I ran faster, my breathing ragged and my chest heaving. "Raj!"

When I reached him, I threw my arms around his shoulders and collapsed in his arms, my legs completely becoming so heavy that I could barely stand anymore. Raj caught me in his arms and lifted me up, pulling me into the same underground prison filled with silver that Kylo had.

Glancing around the prison, I finally scrambled back to my feet and winced at the sudden pressure and thoughts rushing through my mind. I needed to get back as soon as possible, and I needed the entire Lycans pack to come with me.

I didn't trust myself.

"We have to go now," I said, hurrying toward the exit. "We need to get back to Kylo's pack before something terrible happens to him and Roman. Something isn't right. I think Dolus is trying to control me too."

If I gave him control, I was done for.

"We can't leave," Raj said.

"We have to!" I shouted, my voice changing into an intense, scolding presence.

Which scared even me.

I didn't recognize my own voice.

Raj placed his hands on my shoulders, calming me down. "We can't."

I pressed my trembling lips together. "Why not?"

After a couple moments, Raj led me to a silver prison cage, where an older woman stood, her gray hair about to fall out and her teeth barely there. Something about her seemed so eerily familiar.

"Who is this?" I asked, brows furrowing.

"You know who I am," she said.

"The goddess from the party you attended with Kylo. She was an imposter."

My eyes widened as she struggled against the chains. The veins in her eyes glowed a black color, the blood in her cheeks becoming brighter and brighter by the second.

I stared at her and shook my head. "No … it can't be."

"I told you and Dolus that this would never work," she said. "The free will of your wolves is too strong. You will never break Isabella or Roman, two of the strongest wolves in all of the forest. You and Dolus will never be able to be together again, so drop this idea."

I didn't understand what she was saying or *why* she was saying this to me. It didn't make sense in the slightest to the logical me, but … someone inside of me recognized her voice and her body—*her.*

"It will work," I said without meaning to.

"You and Dolus are fools," she said. "They are stronger than you think. No matter who you are to them, you will never break their will, like I've told you from the beginning. You will no longer be able to be with the man you love for eternity. The stories have been diluted with your lies. Your love isn't even alive in the myths anymore. Your history with my brother has been defeated."

"I will kill you," I found myself saying, lunging for the silver bars and taking hold of them. Raj grabbed my waist to pull me back, but I ripped myself out of his hold. "I will end you and be with him. You've never liked us together! Never!"

"Try to stop me all you want. If they trap you here and torture you too, you'll die for good this time. And there will be no coming back from that. You and Dolus will forever be parted from this world. How are you going to change the world this time, Moon Goddess?"

CHAPTER 43

ISABELLA

"What did you just say?" I whispered.

"You were never enough for my brother," the goddess said. "You say that he's corrupted you, but it's you who has corrupted him with the promise of eternity. You make promises that you can't keep and have him hoping that one day, you can be together on the dark side of the moon, but you'd never be able to keep him happy for eternity."

I stared at her in shock and glanced over at Raj, who looked just as taken aback as me.

"Are you saying that the Moon Goddess is inside Isabella?" Raj asked.

"Yes," the goddess said, glaring at me. "I'm not hiding your secrets anymore. I'm not dying for this either."

"What do you mean, dying?" Raj asked.

"Their spirits are dying." She turned back to me. "This was your last chance at togetherness. You screwed it up. Once the body you reside in decays, then you vanish from this world forever. And I will be fucking glad when that happens. My brother hasn't been the same since he met you."

"That means …" I whispered. "If Roman kills Kylo, Dolus will be gone for good."

The sane Lycan half of me loved the thought of Dolus finally being gone from this world while the Moon Goddess residing inside me loathed the thought of her precious Dolus finally leaving.

"Roman won't be able to kill Dolus," the goddess said. "Dolus will kill him."

And I snapped back and seized control of the Moon Goddess. My will would not break to her, and my Roman wouldn't die to a god who wanted nothing more than the spirit who had hijacked my body. As much as I worshiped the Moon Goddess, she couldn't even materialize into a form.

She had taken my body while Dolus had broken Kylo's spirit and taken his.

Not fucking happening.

"What else do we need to know?" Raj asked.

I desperately held back the Moon Goddess, who was clawing on my insides and begging me to release control of my own body for her selfish needs. And I fucking hated the thought of her using me.

She was supposed to be my fucking goddess.

I had worshiped her for years.

Who knew she'd be the biggest fucking bitch I would come to know?

"The only way to stop this craziness is to kill one of them," the goddess spoke. "The other will go insane, but this fucking madness and chaos will be over."

"Come on, Raj!" I shouted. "We need to get to Kylo's pack."

There was only one thing left to do: either kill Kylo to stop this madness or kill myself to stop the Moon Goddess. It seemed, somehow, they were both trapped in our bodies and either couldn't or wouldn't leave us.

But I didn't want to kill Kylo, just to kill Dolus.

And I didn't want to kill myself. I had a fucking pup to birth and raise.

I had to find Roman and Kylo and figure out a plan before they killed each other. And I would need to stay in control the entire time because when I had left Roman and Kylo, it had seemed like Kylo had lost complete control of himself and surrendered to Dolus.

CHAPTER 44

KYLO

*I*sabella was here.

She ran down the prison steps, screaming, her feet hitting the ground hard and fast. She sprinted into the room, shaking her head and shouting at us to stop it now, that we were being controlled not only by Dolus, but the Moon Goddess too, that we needed to come up with a plan to stop this.

But even on her way here, she hadn't come up with a plan to save us.

My body wouldn't stop fighting Roman. I had lost control ten minutes ago, and Roman had been keeping up with my attacks. I couldn't just stop and come up with a plan that probably wouldn't work in the fucking slightest. I had to keep fighting Roman and get rid of Dolus from this world for fucking good.

"Isabella, stay back!" Roman said to her.

Knowing Isabella, I knew she wouldn't. Even more, she wouldn't be able to give me the flower.

Deep down, I knew that once she found out what was really going on, she would try to stop it, like she usually did. And while she would probably succeed, who knew who she would be

171

putting in danger? She might die. Roman might die. Their pup might die.

And I fucking refused to take away Isabella's happiness again.

So, as Dolus had taken control of my body, I had been stepping closer and closer to the back room while fighting Roman. I'd pretended to give Dolus total control and moved back into the room where the flower had been crushed up into that glass.

What I hadn't told Roman before though was that a single flake had fallen on the ground under my desk when he barged into my prison. If Isabella wouldn't give me that fucking drink or I couldn't force myself to drink it while Dolus was in control, I could sneak the leaf into my mouth when he wasn't paying attention.

"Please, stop!" Isabella shouted. "Please!"

"Do it," I howled at Roman, wanting him to tell Isabella what needed to happen.

"Isabella," Roman growled, slashing me in the rib cage. "Grab the glass and force it into Kylo's mouth on my command."

Isabella stared at him with wide eyes and grabbed the glass. "Why? What's in it?"

Roman clenched his jaw and thrust me against the table. "Just do it."

"What's in it, Roman?"

Roman's canines dripped with saliva. "The flower."

Isabella's eyes widened, and she dropped the glass, spilling it everywhere. "No! We can fix this, Roman. We can take control of these gods and goddesses. We can survive together. I'm not going to kill him."

Roman slammed his fist into my jaw and thrust me to the ground. My head banged against the cement, a bruise forming on the back of my head. The leaf lay inches from me, and I told myself that I might be a weak man, but I wasn't going to be anymore.

I would do this for the greater good.

"I'm sorry, Isabella." I grabbed the leaf, stuck it into my mouth, and swallowed. "This is the only way."

"Kylo!" Isabella screamed, dropping to her knees and sticking her fingers into my mouth, desperately trying to fish out the poisonous leaf, but it had already infiltrated my body, broken up in my stomach, and was spreading through every vessel in my body. She shook her head. "No! Spit it out! Kylo!"

"Take care of her," I said to Roman, my throat suddenly closing. "Please."

Roman frowned and nodded, his brows furrowed together in a pained expression. While we might've had our differences, he was still that same kid I used to hang out with and grow stronger with. Old friends might have grown apart, but there would always be that connection.

My body suddenly felt weak, my arms and legs heavy.

"Don't talk like this!" Isabella screamed. "You're not going to d-die. Please, Kylo, you have to stay with us. I'm sorry. I'm so sorry that I couldn't stop this, that I was rude to you these past few days."

"One day, Isabella ..." I whispered, my voice hoarse and my mouth beyond dry. I used all the strength I had left to lift my hand and gently grasp her face, my fingers trembling. "We'll meet again, and I promise you that I'll make you the happiest damn woman alive."

Isabella grasped my hand and held it against her warm face. Tears poured down her flushed cheeks and onto my hand, running down my arm and igniting the last flame I had inside of me. Those tears were the last things I felt as the feeling dimmed from my fingertips, down my hands, and soon my entire body.

"Don't leave us," Isabella pleaded, hovering over me. She placed her hands on my shoulders and gently shook me, her voice fading from above very slowly. "Please, don't leave, Kylo. Please ..."

I stared up at her, my touch and my hearing completely gone

and my sight fading quickly too. I couldn't move my arms or my legs or any part of my body. Instead, I looked at her and Roman for as long as I could, wishing things had gone differently.

Roman knelt beside Isabella, lips curled into a frown and hands around Isabella's shoulders to try to pull her away from my perishing body. She yanked herself out of his hold and shouted something at him, the vein in her neck pulsing wildly and tears gushing from her eyes.

"I love you," I said, but I couldn't hear my own voice, so I didn't know if it had come out right or if she understood me. "I love you so much."

Isabella tensed and gazed down at me, eyes widening and lips trembling. She doubled over me, her body violently shaking back and forth, and her mouth moving to say the same words that I had said. *I love you.*

My eyes became too heavy to keep open, but I held them apart for another moment. When I closed my eyes, darkness flooded around me, suffocating me to the very end. With my breathing heavy, I inhaled as hard as I could to inhale the scent of this world one last time.

Isabella's aroma drifted through my nostrils, filling me and warming me in places that I had never experienced before. Whether Dolus had been attracting me to her or not, she always smelled sweet to me. She had that smell that I'd always remember, even in the afterlife.

And at the very last moment, Isabella kissed me on the lips. I could barely feel it, but her odor coasted into my mouth and gave me hope that one day, one life, I would get to see her bright smile again, just like I had seen that night at the Wolf Moon party.

CHAPTER 45

ISABELLA

While I cried over Kylo, Dolus—nothing but a weak, fragile white aura—drifted out from his body and appeared in front of us. I glanced back at Roman with tears in my eyes and stood in front of him.

"You're not taking Roman too," I said to Dolus.

"My love," he said to me, his words like the wind.

Suddenly, a piercing pain shot through my body from my chest. A black aura slithered out of me and fabricated in front of Dolus. The pair stared at each other for mere moments before Dolus shook his head.

"If you leave her body, then you will die too, my love," Dolus's fading aura said.

"Then, let me die," the Moon Goddess said. "I refuse to live this life without you."

The Moon Goddess embraced Dolus, wrapping her spirit-like arms around his body and pulling him closer to her until they nearly combined as one. If I hadn't just gone through absolute hell, trying to fight their asses, then I would've thought it was actually heartwarming.

But fuck that.

They both deserved to vanish forever.

As quickly as they had emerged from our bodies, their auras faded, their mist drifting off into the darkness of Kylo's prison, their spirits dwindling into nothingness. And just like that, the Moon Goddess, who I had worshiped since I was a young pup, vanished from this world.

With wide eyes, I looked at the space they'd once inhabited. Shock ran through my body.

They were gone.

Truly gone.

"Nobody can know that the Moon Goddess we all worship is dead," I whispered.

I stared down at Kylo's body and balled my hands into fists, tears pricking the corners of my eyes. Multiple people had lost their lives for that bitch, including Kylo, a strong alpha who was loved by his pack.

Maybe I loved him. Maybe I didn't.

Right now, I didn't know what was right from what was wrong, what was truth from what was lie. Did I have two pups inside me, one fathered by Roman, the other by Kylo? Were we ever divine wolves? Was that just a story the Moon Goddess, Dolus, and his sister had fabricated, so we'd believe it? Who knew?

What I did know was that part of Kylo would always be with me.

Roman placed his hand on my shoulder and squeezed tightly. "Nobody."

Deciding that I wouldn't shed any more tears for Kylo— though I so desperately wanted to cry my eyes out and hold him one last time—I turned away from him and walked out of the prison without looking back once.

Kylo might've died, but we'd saved the werewolf species from corruption. We'd stopped a war before it could turn this forest into ruins. Through the death of one strong wolf, we had accomplished peace.

Kylo had accomplished peace.

"Let's go home, Roman," I said, grabbing his hand and walking through the forest, my stomach in tight knots. I wanted to see how Vanessa, Derek, and Roman's sister, Jane, were doing now that this was all over. They had received the worst of Dolus's backlash, and I hoped that the corruption had been reversed now that he was gone. But that wasn't all. "I want to finally rest, so we can prepare for the arrival of our pup—or pups. We deserve it."

EPILOGUE

ISABELLA

ONE MONTH LATER

"I miss him," Roman said, sitting on the porch steps and staring out into the darkening forest. The sun had begun setting nearly an hour ago, the sky already a dark blue. Roman balled his hands into fists and shook his head. "I fucking miss him."

I sat down beside him, cradling my belly bump in one hand and grasping his with my other. "We did what we had to do. We needed to let him go for the sake of humanity and for the sake of … us."

To my surprise, Roman had taken Kylo's death the worst.

After spending the days with our recovering friends and family, Roman sat outside the packhouse every night on these steps and stared out into the woods, as if he was waiting for Kylo to walk into the clearing and throw some vile words in his direction. And while I didn't understand it, I usually sat with him in silence.

"He was my best friend for so many years. He trained me,

mentored me, fucking fought with me," Roman said, shaking his head. "I fucked him over so many fucking times when I was young and immature. We were finally starting to get along, and those gods had to fuck it up."

"It's okay, Roman," I whispered.

"I just wanted us to be good again before either of us left this world."

Instead of responding, I let Roman vent to me. He didn't want me to answer him with logic of any kind. He just wanted someone to talk to, to cry to if he needed it. And when I'd let him mark me, I'd promised to be that woman for him.

Finally, Roman wrapped his arms around my waist and rested his head on my shoulder. I placed my hand over his, closed my eyes, and smiled softly.

"If we really are the divine wolves, then we'll meet again in another life, but right now, we should focus on us and the future."

Roman kissed my ear and ran his hand over my growing belly. "And our baby."

"Babies," I whispered.

"Babies?" Roman asked, pulling away slightly and smiling. "Babies?!"

"My mom confirmed it today. I have two of those suckers growing inside me."

"Well, I'd better start on dinner then." He placed another kiss on my cheek and hopped up from the stairs, heading toward our front door. "A feast for four tonight. And don't you move an inch. I'll bring it out to you."

When the front door snapped shut, I grinned.

Who knew me having pups would whip that man into shape?

A tree branch snapped in the distance, and I glanced up, spotting a wolf watching me. My chest tightened at the sight of those piercing gold eyes, and I stopped breathing for a couple moments.

Oh my goodness.

No.

This isn't real.

Before I knew it, I shot up from the stairs and ran toward the forest, where I swore I had seen him. But when I reached the area, there was no wolf and no smell in sight. Instead, a glowing white moonflower sat in its place.

My favorite flower.

THE END...
For now.

WHILE THIS TRILOGY might be over, some of these characters will reappear in The Twins! You can order it here: https:// books2read.com/the-twins A couple of your burning questions about Isabella, Roman, and Kylo just might be answered ;)

ABOUT THE AUTHOR

Emilia Rose is an international best-selling author of steamy paranormal romance. Highly inspired by her study abroad trip to Greece in 2019, Emilia loves to include Greek and Roman mythology in her writing.

She graduated from the University of Pittsburgh with a degree in psychology and a minor in creative writing in 2020 and now writes novels as her day job.

With over 18 million combined story views online and a growing presence on reading apps, she hopes to inspire other young novelists with her story of growth and imagination, so they go on to write the stories that need to be told.

STAY CONNECTED

Subscribe to Emilia's newsletter for exclusive news >
https://www.emiliarosewriting.com/

Printed in Great Britain
by Amazon

15251625R00109